About the Author

Although he was born in London, Robert's family emigrated to New Zealand when he was eleven. Robert worked for forty years as an engineer, where he initially used his creativity on mechanically related projects. As time went by, Robert was eventually persuaded by his friends and family to start turning some of the many plots that he had developed over the years into meaningful, written dialogue, including this novel, *The Mason Pact*.

robertgordonauthor.com

THE MASON PACT

Robert Gordon

THE MASON PACT

Vanguard Press

VANGUARD PAPERBACK

© Copyright 2024
Robert Gordon

The right of Robert Gordon to be identified as author of this work has been asserted by him in accordance with the Copyright, Designs and Patents Act 1988.

All Rights Reserved

No reproduction, copy or transmission of this publication may be made without written permission.
No paragraph of this publication may be reproduced, copied or transmitted save with the written permission of the publisher, or in accordance with the provisions of the Copyright Act 1956 (as amended).

Any person who commits any unauthorised act in relation to this publication may be liable to criminal prosecution and civil claims for damages.

A CIP catalogue record for this title is available from the British Library.

ISBN 978 1 80016 837 4

Vanguard Press is an imprint of
Pegasus Elliot Mackenzie Publishers Ltd.
www.pegasuspublishers.com

This is a work of fiction. Names, characters, businesses, places, events and incidents are either the products of the author's imagination or used in a fictitious manner. Any resemblance to actual persons, living or dead, or actual events is purely coincidental.

First Published in 2024

Vanguard Press
Sheraton House Castle Park
Cambridge England

Printed & Bound in Great Britain

Chapter 1

Late September 1997

The damp cold penetrated mercilessly through to his bones as Matt moved his left arm just enough to look at his watch. It was one minute past two. Moving his hand slowly back to its original position, he resumed holding his wife, Nancy, close to his side for both comfort and warmth.

The broken windows of the now long-abandoned farmhouse were unable to stop the chilling breeze that reverberated around the empty space of what had become their makeshift bedroom for the night. The wind showed no mercy as it relentlessly swayed the trees that stood adjacent to the derelict building. These same trees cast an eerie shadow from the moonlight on the building's bare internal walls. The erratically moving shadows were images that, if left unchecked, could play havoc with a person's imagination.

Despite the fact they were both mentally and physically exhausted, too many things had happened over the past few days to allow them the luxury of a peaceful night's rest. The cause of their anxiety was that the circumstances they would be stepping into later that morning had unknown consequences. Although they both felt good about the upcoming day and the decisions they would need to make, they did not know for sure if their chosen path would bring incarceration or freedom. Would it be an end to the torment and uncertainty of their current situation? Or would it be the start of something far worse?

For Nancy, the nightmare had started just over six and three-quarter years earlier, when Matt's true past was finally revealed to her. There were many secrets Nancy was yet to discover – some that Matt had been concealing since they first met; the rest he himself was totally unaware of and would not have guessed even in his wildest dreams. However, it was also fair to say that Nancy had been holding onto her own secrets, and just like Matt's, her secrets had been kept closely guarded for very good reasons. Had either of their secrets been exposed, the potential result would have destroyed them both.

For Matt, the sequence of events that led to where they now found themselves had begun much earlier: three months short of thirty-two years, to be exact. For many reasons, December 1965 was truly a lifetime ago, when, as a naive young man of seventeen, he was living in a small town called Mason.

When viewed on a map, Mason looked to be not physically far from where they now found themselves sheltering that cold, windy night. However, the Mason where Matt grew up might as well have been a million miles away, for back then, he was living a very different life in a very different world.

Chapter 2

December 1965 (thirty-two years ago)

Any reputable movie company looking to portray a typical American town would find it epitomised in the township of Mason, Ohio. With a population that hovered around the fifteen-thousand mark, everything about Mason was proudly American, and nowhere was this more evident than at the war memorial dedicated to its fallen sons. The four-sided obelisk that listed all one hundred and fifty-two of Mason's former inhabitants sat upon a gleaming marble foundation that was surrounded by a bright green carpet of neatly manicured lawn. The obelisk stood at the apex of a triangular section of ground, where the aptly named Main Street divided, with the right-hand roadway becoming Cherry Street. Encircling the grass edges of the memorial was a white picket fence that bordered the concrete footpath; its purpose was to deter anyone from doing the unthinkable by taking a shortcut across this hallowed ground.

Only two things gave Mason an originality that distinguished it from other similarly sized towns. One was the Carlsson Orphanage, a large English manor-style building that stood on the western outskirts; the other was the magnificent fireworks display held every New Year's Eve, a tradition that stretched back over one hundred years. Despite Mason's relatively small size, this annual event had made the town famous throughout most of the state. The display always drew large crowds from not only the town but also the surrounding districts.

It was this very event that found five young friends sitting on the steps of Mason's courthouse on this cool last day of 1965. The close friends were eagerly awaiting the festivities that the evening promised. Little did they know that tonight would change their destinies, eventually turning them into fugitives from everything they had ever known.

The hands of the town hall clock rolled around to eight o'clock, still four hours before the fireworks display. The entertainment, however, had begun at six o'clock, and the elevated position of the courthouse steps made for a good vantage point, being at least eight feet above the heads of the crowd that were now swelling below them.

Matt Brown sat one step higher than his four companions, his eyes slowly surveying the sea of faces comprising the heavy crowd below. He was aware that many of Mason's citizens would consider themselves privileged when compared to Matt and his friends. From a third-party perspective, all of those souls may have appeared, in some ways, to have a lot more in their lives, but so much of that was surely only superficial. In contrast, what Matt had was immeasurable. As he looked over his four friends seated below, he knew he was extremely lucky. Those four young people were not just any friends, but were, in fact, the best four friends in the world.

Jenny was the oldest of the five. She was almost eighteen and potentially a very pretty girl. 'Potentially' was the most appropriate word because she had never allowed herself the privilege of being pretty. Her hair was always cut short, no makeup had ever adorned her face and her choice of clothes would have better suited a boy of her age. Yet, despite her tomboy appearance, there was no doubt that her fine facial features and warm smile gave a glimpse of the beauty that she had tried so hard to hide from the outside world. It was not only Jenny's appearance that made her a tomboy but also the fact that she could run, swim, climb and kick a ball equally as well as any of the boys she played with. Jenny had never allowed the fact that she was a girl prevent her from competing in any sport she set her mind on, including a few that, up to that time, were a male-only domain in her school. In many ways, Jenny was different to the other four who sat on the steps that night, but there was one thing that she and the others had in common. From an outsider's viewpoint, their camaraderie was the result of quite a sad fact. Maybe there was some truth to that, but life's circumstances had, for them, resulted in the forging of a strong bond of friendship and loyalty. They were all orphans and residents of the Carlsson Orphanage.

Every person, past or present, who had resided at the orphanage was familiar with the story of how this very English, aristocratic-looking building came to be. It all went back to the late 1880s, when a wealthy English landowner, Robert Worthington, brought his young bride, Cecilia, across the Atlantic to join him in his new home in Mason. Believing that a taste of familiarity was the cure for his wife's homesickness, Robert proceeded to have Worthington Hall built at a great cost.

An army of local labourers overseen by skilled English craftsmen, each commissioned by and brought to the States by Robert Worthington, collectively toiled long days for over a two-year period. Each person executed their individual skills to build, together, the monumental structure that rose gallantly from the barren earth.

Reminiscent of an English manor house, Worthington Hall appeared many years older than its actual age. The ornate brickwork encapsulated the large multi-pane windows, each of which had been shipped from Hamptons, the renowned glaziers in Bristol, England. Several chimney stacks comprising part of the exterior brickwork rose from ground level to above the roofline, each servicing two fireplaces, one on each level.

Behind the solid entrance doors, a wide, oak staircase rose to the upper floor and its eight large bedrooms. Further skywards, inside the slope of the roof cavity, were the servants' quarters, where each member of the staff was allocated a small but comfortable room containing a single bed and freestanding wardrobe. The servants' quarters were accessed only by two internal staircases, both at the back of the house and hidden from the view of any guests.

Worthington Hall was, indeed, overkill for a young couple, but driven by a misguided belief that living in a house reminiscent of her childhood upbringing would quell his wife's desire to return to England, Robert Worthington pressed ahead with its elaborate construction.

As magnificent a structure as the finished erection was, it seemed so out of place in its American landscape. A more fitting location would have been a wooded English countryside. Now, nearly eighty years later, Worthington Hall was still a proud testament to the skilled craftsmen that Robert Worthington had brought across the Atlantic from England. However, its name and purpose had now changed, a consequence of the troubled lives of the Worthington family.

Unable to conceive and still terribly homesick, Cecilia Worthington suffered badly from depression, and it was one cold day in late December 1899 that she was found floating, face down, in the local river. Whether it was an accident or suicide was irrelevant to a devastated Robert Worthington. He returned to England a broken man, never to set foot on American soil again. For the next twenty years, Worthington Hall fell into a state of disrepair; eventually, it was sold by the trustees of the Worthington estate to a Swedish God-fearing gentleman, Carlo Carlsson. At that point, Worthington Hall became the Carlsson Orphanage.

Since its opening in 1921, the Carlsson Orphanage had helped many parentless children get a good start in life. Life at the orphanage followed a strict regime under the direct guidance of Carlo Carlsson himself until his death in 1955, when the home was transferred to his nephew Herbert, who dedicated his life to following the legacy of his late uncle in caring for the county's most needy young citizens. Herbert Carlsson's second-in-command and closest confidante was old Mrs Appleton. She was also the closest person that any resident of the orphanage would get to a motherly figure. No one knew exactly how old she actually was; the children's estimates ranged anywhere from sixty-five to an unrealistic three hundred years. Regardless of her exact age, Mrs Appleton was a feisty individual who took no nonsense from anybody. However, underneath her hard exterior shell, was a kind, loving person on whom Herbert Carlsson relied heavily to help make sure the orphanage ran smoothly.

The orphanage's policies were simple: if you were parentless or had been abandoned, you would be taken in, clothed, fed and educated at the local school. In return, you were expected to obey the rules of the orphanage, attend school every day and actively help by tending the farm animals and assisting with the fruit and vegetable plots whose spoils fed the staff and residents. Surplus produce was sold on the orphanage's behalf by Jerry's Grocers on Main Street. Anyone who had been taken in by the orphanage could leave once they reached the age of fifteen, but they were encouraged to stay until eighteen. After their sixteenth birthday, residents were expected to obtain a part-time job, with all the earnings paid directly to the orphanage. This, plus the proceeds from the sale of the produce, as well as donations from local businesses and interest from investments made by the Carlsson Trust, kept the orphanage running. Upon reaching the age of eighteen, residents were given a small monetary sum from the previous two years' earnings and the freedom to face the world on their own.

Jenny had been at the orphanage for most of her seventeen and three-quarters years, just like her two friends, Matt and Adam. Only a couple of months separated the birthdays of the two boisterous young men, although Matt's exact birthday was never known because he was left at the orphanage in the dead of night, wrapped in an old, blue blanket inside a wicker bassinette, with no indication of who he was or where he was from. The staff estimated that he was about four-weeks old. Adam had arrived at the orphanage six weeks later, at barely two-weeks old. His desperate mother had said that she could not afford to keep him as her husband had been killed in a farming accident, and with no home or job, she was struggling to feed herself, let alone provide for a young baby.

Matt and Adam had effectively grown up as brothers. Although they did not share a single drop of the same blood, they had often been mistaken for twins, not so much because of their looks but because their mannerisms, conversations and unspoken bond had always kept them close. They knew each other well, including each other's strengths and weaknesses. This had made for a very competitive environment, with each trying hard to be just that bit quicker, nimbler or smarter than the other.

Next in age was Christine – the very lovely, beautiful Christine, with fair skin, long, flowing, blonde hair, warm smile and big, captivating, blue eyes which, with a direct look, would stop any boy in his tracks. Every girl wanted to be Christine, and every boy wanted to be with Christine. Both Matt and Adam guarded her like two protective older brothers, but despite any prospective suitor needing to get past them first, any effort would have been wasted as Christine had no desire for anything beyond totally platonic friendships. She had turned up at the orphanage at the age of three, dropped off by her grandmother, who had cared for her since her parents had died. Christine had been smartly dressed, and her grandmother had pinned twenty dollars to her pink coat.

"The money is all I have. Please look after her," sobbed the old lady as she slowly walked away, her eyes spilling with tears.

Julian was the youngest of the five. You could not help but feel pity for the slightly built, seventeen-year-old boy, who had a speech impediment and pronounced limp that had totally destroyed his social confidence. His physical injuries were the result of being thrown from his parents' car after it had been hit by a freight train on a level crossing. No seat belt, a door that flung open and a shallow ditch combined to be instrumental in his survival. The accident had left his right leg so badly mangled that the doctors said he was lucky to still have the use of it. As there was nothing physically limiting Julian's speech, the doctors had assumed it was the shock of being trapped in the ditch while watching his parents burn in the wreckage of their car that caused it. Julian would never talk about what he witnessed that day, but he was always visibly distressed at the sound of any scream, even a playful one.

Although Julian had all the attributes to be targeted by bullies, the few who had tried had soon suffered the consequences. If you messed with Julian, then Matt and Adam would mess with you. Worse still was if you were unlucky enough to pick on Julian when Jenny was around. Matt and Adam knew when to stop; they knew when the perpetrator had learnt his lesson. Jenny, however, did not. She guarded Julian so fiercely that anyone foolish enough to pick on him would endure a severe beating that would end only when she was physically pulled off. One such incident had caused a major rift between the orphanage and the school that took almost six months to resolve.

As the minutes ticked by, more and more people arrived from not only the surrounding county but also from further afield, such was the reputation of Mason's New Year's Eve celebrations. County Park, two blocks down on Cherry Street, was where it would all happen, and just like the preceding years, at around eleven o'clock, folks would start walking down to stake their position for the display. But with the time now just after eight o'clock, most of the activity was still taking place on Main Street up to its intersection with Cherry Street. The delicious smells of warm nuts, cotton candy, candy apples, hamburgers and hot dogs mingled as they rose from the stalls below and slowly drifted up the steps, making the five friends drool. But with no money between them, it only served to induce a small amount of envy for those children walking around with their parents who seemed to be frequently opening their wallets. The barely audible rumbling of Matt's stomach reminded them that the next time they would be eating wasn't until tomorrow morning's breakfast.

"Listen," said Jenny, trying to break the gloom. "I have something I want to show you; something that is better than stupid old cotton candy."

"What is it, Jenny?" Adam asked, curious.

"No, no, no. You must wait and see. But it is something nice; something better than the food stalls. We have to take a short walk. So who's coming, then?" Jenny quickly stood up and walked down the first three steps before stopping to look around and see who was following. Her sudden halt nearly caused a human pile-up on the steps as all four of her friends were right behind her, eager to see what could possibly be better than hot dogs and cotton candy.

Jenny led them along the side of the courthouse and down a narrow alleyway that separated the building from the town hall, and then, turning behind a low fence, they followed a small path around a corner and down half a dozen steps. A solid wooden door blocked further access, but a bit of fiddling with the lock by Jenny soon had it open.

"Follow me," she said excitedly as she led her friends down a short passageway to the dark space underneath the steps they had just been sitting on. Flicking a switch enabled a dusty bulb to produce a dull incandescent glow, barely illuminating the gloomy area.

"Wow!" exclaimed Adam. "This is amazing! I never knew this place existed."

"I don't think many people do. It's almost like a secret place, but I still have my surprise for you all, so close your eyes, and don't open them until I say." Four pairs of eyes nervously closed, awaiting Jenny's surprise. "Okay – you can open them now."

Opened eyes revealed that Jenny was holding three bottles of wine. One was unopened, but the label was missing. The other two had been opened and a small amount consumed before the corks had been replaced.

"Wine! But I've never drunk wine before. Where did you get them from?" Christine looked shocked.

The truth of the matter was that residing at the orphanage and the consequential limitations had never allowed any of the friends to have contact with alcohol in any form prior to their leaving.

"It's okay, Christine. I got them from work. They were going to get thrown out."

Since turning sixteen, Jenny had worked part-time at Mrs Cooper's restaurant on Cherry Street, progressing from kitchen washer to serving staff. She was well regarded by the other staff and customers alike. She had rescued the three bottles of wine which could not be sold and were going to be tipped down the drain. Just like all the other residents of the orphanage in the sixteen-to-eighteen-year-old age group, Jenny never saw any of her wages.

"Here, try some, Christine. I'm sure you'll like it. I've tried it at work a few times when a little has been left in a bottle. I only have two glasses, so we'll have to share." Jenny pulled out two glasses and a corkscrew she had borrowed from work and concealed in an old cupboard, where she had also hidden the wine. The glasses were passed around, allowing four inquisitive mouths to sample the contents, and both glasses soon needed refilling. The transformation of the group, who were not used to even a small amount of alcohol, would have been apparent to anyone except themselves. Even Julian was laughing. The conversation became louder and soon turned to what the upcoming year held for them all.

"There's something I need to tell you all," Jenny interrupted.

"What is it, Jenny?" Christine questioned.

"As you know, I will be turning eighteen in February and have to leave the orphanage. What you don't know is that I'm leaving Mason as well."

Adam's voice broke the silence. "You're what? Where are you going?"

"I'm going to Paris. Jean Michel has asked me to come live with him and his parents. He also asked me to marry him, and I said yes."

Jean Michel was a French exchange student who had spent four months at Mason County School the previous year. None of Jenny's friends could understand the attraction between them. He was the total opposite of everything that Jenny was. Always immaculately dressed and groomed, Jean Michel had an air of femininity about him, and although he did participate in a few sports during his stay at the school, he was most content just sitting quietly and writing poetry. Even though it totally baffled most people, Matt and Adam in particular, there was no doubt that there was a strong attraction between him and Jenny. The attraction was not instantaneous, but it was one that seemed to grow each day during his stay in Mason. After his return to France, Jean Michel and Jenny had kept in contact, writing to each other regularly. Jenny's news now left the rest speechless and gaping in disbelief.

"Well, aren't you pleased for me, then?" Jenny seemed a bit taken aback by the silence.

Christine, realising the awkwardness, broke the silence. "Of course, we are, Jenny. It's just such a surprise. We never thought about you leaving Mason, let alone America, and I am going to miss you so much."

"Are you really going to marry... him?" As soon as he heard the words leave his mouth, Adam realised how bad it sounded and quickly went into damage control. "I meant that... um, I'm surprised you're leaving us," he stammered unconvincingly.

"I know what you meant, Adam, and I know exactly what you and Matt are thinking. But let me tell you that it was fate that brought us together. Paris, France, and Mason, Ohio; it's no coincidence that we met. I know he's a bit different from you, but there's a side to him that you don't know. He has a sensitive soul and knows just what I'm thinking. What he's offered me is a once-in-a-lifetime opportunity. I know he can give me something I might never have the chance to experience again. I love him, and he loves me."

"I'm sorry, Jenny. I truly wish you all the best; I really do. I want you to be happy," Adam said sheepishly.

"Me too, Jenny. I wish you a happy life, and I'm sure you'll love Paris. You'll be able to practise your French full time." Matt had finally managed to speak.

"Thank you both. It means a lot to me." Jenny turned to Julian, who had been very quiet. She could see he was smiling, but his eyes were filled with tears. She stepped forward to hug him.

"You will all look after Julian for me, won't you?"

"Of course," came the combined reply.

Jenny hugged all of her friends, saving the longest for Julian, as the conversation turned to what the future may hold for her in France and indeed the others, as they progressively turned eighteen and, one by one, had to leave the orphanage and possibly Mason, as well.

They all knew that when Jenny left in a few weeks' time, it would probably be the last time they would all be together. They talked about how they would keep in touch and how they could all meet up in the future. It was Matt who hatched the plan.

"Hey, guys – I hope we do all keep in touch and meet up regularly," he said. "But let's also make a plan, just in case, if for some reason, we do lose contact in the future and end up going our separate ways."

"I'm sure we won't lose contact; we mustn't let that happen."

"And I'm sure of that, as well. But we just don't know what life will throw at us. Some of us, like Jenny, might end up overseas or maybe just out of state. Yes, we must plan to keep in touch, but despite our best intentions, there might be reasons we can't; maybe reasons beyond our control that make a group catch-up impossible. We need a backup plan – a plan that can't fail, even if all else does, and one that we are one hundred per cent committed to, so that no matter what happens in our lives, good or bad or whatever, we will know, inside, that one day, we will definitely all meet up again."

"Sounds good, Matt. But what did you have in mind?" Jenny questioned.

"Well... how about... tonight, right now, we all agree that no matter what happens in our lives, we'll meet here in, say, twenty-five years. Just the five of us – no wives, no husbands, no children and no other friends. Just us."

"Twenty-five years! That's a lifetime away! Why not five or ten?" Adam queried.

"You're right, Adam. It is a lifetime away, but there's a reason I made it that long. I'm sure we'll keep in contact and see each other next year, and in five years, and in ten years and so on. It will obviously be a lot harder to catch up with Jenny, but we can all still keep in contact. She can write to us, and we can write back to her. And on special occasions, we can always phone.

"But none of us knows what life is going to put in our path. We might get married and have lots of children. There might be another war and one of us gets captured as a prisoner. Maybe one of us even goes to jail for a crime they didn't commit because of mistaken identity."

Christine winced. "I certainly hope not."

"Me too. I was just using that as an example of why one or more of us might lose contact with the others. We're certainly not planning to drift apart, and we must make every attempt to stop that from happening, but if for some reason someone does, then we have a plan that cannot fail. We'll always know that there's a time when we can all meet up again. It's important that we don't tell anyone – and I do mean anybody! We must not write the details down anywhere or talk about our plan just in case someone sees or hears and wants to come along. It'll be a secret that only five people in the world know about, the five of us. Let's do this right now; we commit that on 31 December 1990, on the steps of the courthouse, we will all meet up, regardless of where in the world we are or whatever our circumstances. We will then come back under here and have a glass of wine just like we are now. So, what do you think? Shall we do it?" Matt thrust his hand out.

"Count me in." Jenny grasped Matt's wrist.

"Me too," exclaimed Adam.

Christine piped up. "And me."

"Yes, I'll be here." Julian's acknowledgement completed the pact as the five hands that had met in the middle gripped the wrist of the person to their right, thus creating a star formation. Matt repeated the information slowly and deliberately so there could be no possibility of confusion. The pact was now made, and they all intended to keep it.

Chapter 3

March 1966 saw Jenny leave for her new life in France, albeit a few weeks late due to difficulties in obtaining her passport. Jean Michel's parents had been wonderful for not only paying for her relocation but also ensuring that her journey went as smoothly as possible, a great help for someone who had never been too far outside of Mason.

March was also a stressful time for both Matt and Adam as the realisation struck home that they would soon be turning eighteen and would have to leave the orphanage, too. But that was not the main issue. They were both very capable boys with good attitudes and work ethics; consequently, they would have no problems making their way in the world. There was, however, one thing holding them both back – it was a deep-seated issue that had put limitations on both their futures, and it was the same predicament that had influenced nearly everything they had done in most of their seventeen-plus years. Both were hopelessly in love with Christine, although neither would admit to it. No romantic interludes had ever taken place between Christine and either boy; to her, they were just the surrogate brothers that she had grown up with. Sadly, for both Matt and Adam, it presented a big problem as neither was willing to make a move for fear of being rejected and consequently allowing the other the opportunity. Both knew that while Christine was in Mason, neither of them could leave to explore the world because it would leave the other behind and give him the chance to be with her.

Matt had worked at Jennings' Hardware Supplies on Main Street since turning sixteen. Old man Jennings had been good to him, and he was well liked by the other workers. Matt knew that he had a job for life, but somehow, the prospect of spending his whole life in Mason had a suffocating feel to it. He was aware that there was a big, undiscovered world outside the town limits, but he'd never been outside the county or the state, let alone the country. But how could he leave? If he did, he would leave Adam and Christine together, and who knows what might happen? All those years of being competitive, trying to be just that little bit better than Adam, in the hope that Christine would notice him as more than just a friend, would have been wasted. If only Christine had been like Jenny and found someone from overseas who could have taken her away and allowed Matt and Adam to get on with their lives. Unfortunately, although Christine could have had any boy that she wanted, she'd never shown any interest in the opposite sex outside of platonic friendship. Matt's only consolation, if you could call it that, was knowing that Adam felt the same way and was in the same predicament.

Adam's after-school job at Wilson's Garage allowed him to be close to his real passion: cars. Working in the forecourt, Adam was employed to pump gas and check oil and water levels for customers. However, his genuine interest in what happened back in the workshop didn't go unnoticed by Ernie Wilson. Ernie had occasionally allowed him to help Hank and Bill with a few basic mechanical tasks. Adam also had a friend in local business owner Buzz Watson. Adam had fallen in love with Buzz's 1961 Dodge Super D/500, a car he thought was the epitome of style, with its sloping rear shape that oozed class. Buzz was a shrewd businessman and had many financial interests around the local area, but the love he shared with Adam was automobiles. He had a collection that was his pride and joy, mostly from the fifties. Several months before, Buzz had invited Adam to do minor jobs on a few of his cars, mainly just washing and waxing, but in return, Buzz gave Adam some driving lessons in the big Dodge along some of the quiet roads on the outskirts of Mason. Attending school, after-school study time and his share of the chores at the orphanage took their toll on the available time Adam had. Added together with his job at the gas station, it was hard to find the time to cycle out to Buzz's farm. However, Adam somehow always managed to find the time to make the long ride there and back, usually on a Saturday or Sunday afternoon.

It was three weeks before Matt's birthday when Herbert Carlsson called him into his office.

"Matt, come on in. I have been meaning to have a chat with you. How is your job at the store going?"

"Very good, thank you, Mr Carlsson."

"I thought as much. I have been hearing some good reports. But that is not the reason I called you in. As we both know, you will be turning eighteen soon, and we will have to say goodbye to you as you make your way in the world. I was wondering what your plans are. Do you think that you will stay here in Mason and keep working at the hardware store, or do you plan to travel?"

"I would like to travel, yes. Perhaps to the East Coast. New York would be amazing; Hawaii would be nice, as well, and maybe even visit Jenny in France. But it's just not practical now. The store can only give me limited hours, so I guess I'll be in Mason for a while till I can save some money."

"So, you would like to travel, then. Well, Matt, anything is possible if you really want it."

"But I haven't got any money; only what I'll get from the orphanage when I leave, so I can't afford to travel. Not yet, anyway." Although this reason was true enough, it was not the main reason that kept him in Mason. How could he move away and leave Adam with Christine? The idea was inconceivable.

"Matt, I may have a solution that would allow you to travel and see some of the country. I was contacted by an old acquaintance recently who now works for a government department that works closely with the military. Anyhow, he is looking for someone just like you. Now, according to what he has briefly told me, you will not actually be in the military, but you will be working closely with both the army and the air force. There will be travel to interesting places available, and evidently, you will be paid very well. So, you would have all the advantages of being enlisted while remaining a civilian. It sounds like a great opportunity, and if you are interested, he would like to meet you and formally make you a job offer. So, what do you think?"

Matt was initially taken aback. It seemed, based on what he had heard so far, to be a great offer, but he just couldn't accept it. But how could he explain his refusal to Mr Carlsson?

"It sounds great, Mr Carlsson. But I can't leave Adam. We've grown up together, and he's like a brother to me. I would miss him." Matt thought that this explanation sounded quite plausible, but he didn't realise that Herbert Carlsson was fully aware of the situation between Matt, Adam and Christine, and he'd been expecting Matt to refuse.

"Matt, there are two opportunities available. The other will be offered to Adam, so if he says yes, would you be interested?"

"I guess so, but Adam isn't eighteen for another two months."

"We will work something out so the two of you can leave together."

Matt smiled. Suddenly, out of the blue, here was the solution to his dilemma. He might not be able to have Christine, but neither would Adam.

Chapter 4

The ten fifteen a.m. bus to Springtown pulled up as it did every weekday, its arrival interrupting Matt and Adam's goodbyes. The boys received a hug from Christine, Julian and some of the others from the orphanage, a handshake and a pat on the back from Herbert Carlsson and farewells from Buzz, Ernie, old man Jennings and all the staff from the hardware store, which had closed down for half an hour. Matt struggled to hold back the tears that were starting to form. Looking directly at Adam would have revealed red watery eyes in return. Matt, however, had no intention of looking at his friend because it would have given away his own emotional state. Even at a time like this, they were still trying to outdo each other, and any hint of a tear would have been a sign of weakness. Matt looked straight ahead as he boarded the bus, stopping only to allow the driver to clip his ticket. As the bus pulled away, their window seats on the right-hand side allowed them to view the sea of waving hands and the only life they had ever known. It was both exciting and scary.

Earlier that morning, the day had started just like any other, with the alarm going off at six. The biggest difference to the previous days was that both boys were wide awake and had been for several hours, as the realisation sank in that this would be the last morning they would wake up in these beds. After dressing and washing, it was downstairs at six forty-five to help set up the dining room for Mrs Appleton's seven o'clock breakfast.

After helping to clean up, there were the final formalities to complete. Taking them aside into a separate room, Herbert Carlsson gave both boys their bank books plus an additional twenty dollars each. He also gave them a letter from Max with all the details of their travel itinerary. Up to this point, they had only known they were heading to Denver, starting with a bus ride to Springtown. Opening the letter revealed two sets of bus tickets, two sets of train tickets, four ten-dollar notes and a neatly written letter, which Adam took in one hand and then passed the other end to Matt so they could jointly read its contents.

Hello Adam and Matt.

Enclosed are all the required tickets for your trip to Denver. Your journey starts with the ten fifteen bus to Springtown. From there, you will go by bus to Cleveland, by train to Chicago and then by train to Denver.

You arrive in Chicago late at night, and your train to Denver is not until six in the morning, but don't go wandering off. Stay in the station and try to get some sleep in the waiting room because the trip from there to Denver will be nearly eighteen hours. I will be there to meet you at the train station in Denver, and we will go over any further details when I see you. Additionally, enclosed is forty dollars to cover the taxi ride in Cleveland and any food, drinks or additional expenses on your journey. The full itinerary is detailed below.

Monday 14 March bus to Springtown bus depot Depart 10:15; arrive 11:00
Monday 14 March bus to Cleveland bus depot Depart 11:40; arrive 14:05
Monday 14 March taxi from Cleveland bus depot to Cleveland railway station
Monday 14 March train to Chicago's Union train station Depart 17:00; arrive 23:55
Tuesday 15 March train to Denver Central Park railway station Depart 06:00; arrive 23:50
I look forward to seeing you both.
Max

Both the boys had made the forty-five minute trip to Springtown several times before to take part in sporting events. Up to now, Springtown had been the furthest they had ever been outside of Mason; anything past Springtown was the start of the big world that lay beyond. Buzz had given Adam a map of central and eastern America, and it was with great enthusiasm that they started to follow their travels on it, marking their progress with a red pen. In the past, the trip to Springtown was a big adventure; maybe even the highlight of the year. Now, the twenty-two or so miles seemed such an insignificant distance compared to the miles that lay ahead.

There would be a forty-minute wait at the bus terminal; just enough time for a drink, toilet stop and quick walk to stretch their legs. Springtown bus terminal would be the changeover point for a bus to Cleveland; from there, the remainder of their journey would be by train. For two young men who had never seen a train, let alone been on one, a combined twenty-five-hour train trip and then a flight on an aeroplane was almost incomprehensible. Boarding the second bus was in many ways a lot easier than the departure from Mason. There would be no teary eyes or the faces of everybody who comprised their de facto family.

This time, Matt made eye contact with the other passengers as he approached the back of the vehicle. With no teary emotions to hide, an overly excited Matt was tempted to ask his fellow travellers if this bus trip was also the start of an adventure in their lives. However, he wisely decided to refrain as it would surely have sounded childish and betray the naivety of his life. This bus was both longer and higher than the first, and in addition, softer seats and bigger windows would make the upcoming two-hour-and-twenty minute trip a more pleasurable and scenic experience. Most of the other passengers already on the bus made little or no effort to return Matt's smile and friendly gestures. A young woman in her early twenties did reciprocate upon Matt's approach; her warm, genuine smile made her face come to life, enhancing her looks. However, as pretty as she was, Matt knew she wasn't and never would be Christine.

Slowly, the small towns and rural landscapes gradually transformed into suburban Cleveland, complete with its increasing population density, until finally, the first distant glimpses of the city's centre became visible, sending an awed feeling through the two small-town boys. Adam reminded Matt that their next stop in Chicago would show them a city that was six times bigger. Matt looked at the map and contemplated Adam's words; he was suddenly hit with a realisation of how big the world was and just how insignificant a town like Mason was, let alone one person from a town so small.

Stepping out of the taxi that had taken them from the bus station to the train station, both Matt and Adam felt a nervous excitement as they walked up the stairs leading to the building's entrance.

Matt mused, "When do you think our adventure actually starts? Leaving Mason? Leaving Springtown? Or right now, as we get ready to board the train?"

Adam thought for a few moments before answering. "Well, I guess anything that is new or brings a sense of excitement or anticipation is an adventure, so all three qualify. Let's say part one of the adventure started in Mason, as the town where we grew up. Part two started when leaving Springtown, because we were going further than we'd ever been before. Part three starts soon, when we get on a train for the first time, and part four starts in Chicago. Part five is in Denver, when we meet up with Max. Goodness knows how many other parts there will be after that. Six, seven, eight, maybe twenty, but regardless of how many parts there are of this adventure, each one will be exciting."

Adam felt he'd just delivered undeniable words of wisdom, and he and Matt clapped hands in the air, complete with a grunt of accomplishment.

The three-hour wait for their train went surprisingly quickly. After surveying where they would have to go to board, Matt led Adam on a small expedition and eventually found a spot that offered an ideal viewing location for observing trains leaving the station.

Matt felt the vibrations from the massive engines reverberate throughout his body as the powerful trains passed close by, straining as they accelerated their heavy loads. Neither Adam nor Matt had ever experienced anything so powerful; the image remained burnt into their memories for many years.

Crossing over the state line into Indiana had been exciting for them both, even though it was mostly symbolic. As the boys were following the train's progress on their map, they had a good idea of when the crossover occurred, but as hard as they looked, there were no signs to indicate it had happened. The first time out of Ohio represented all the excitement that the future held, and there was still Illinois, Iowa and Nebraska to go before they even got to Colorado, the real starting place of their new future lives.

The ambient light had long since disappeared before the first signs of the metropolis that was Chicago became evident. The lights from the inside of the carriage reflected images of the interior in the windows, limiting a clear view of what lay beyond. The boys did note, however, the first signs of the looming city as acres and acres of suburban houses gave way to more densely populated areas before finally succumbing to the crowning glory of the city centre, which, when stared at, glowed against the dark sky like a Christmas tree of immeasurable proportions.

Inside the station, Matt remarked, "Well, there's the waiting room. I guess we should try to get a bit of sleep. I'll set my alarm for five."

Adam had different ideas. "How about we go for a bit of a walk? Just an hour would be fine – enough time to have a quick look. After all, we might never get back here."

Matt was not so sure it was a good idea. "Max specifically said to stay at the station and get some rest."

"I've read about cities like New York and Chicago," Adam insisted, "never thinking I would actually get here. I'm going to go for a walk; you can stay, if you like, and I'll see you when I get back."

Having Adam go exploring on his own seemed like an even worse idea than the two of them going together, so despite his reservations, Matt decided that if Adam was going for a look around, then he should really go, as well.

"Okay. I'll go with you, but an hour maximum. And we will need to put our bags in a locker. I saw some as we walked in. It'll cost us a quarter."

Stepping out of the Union Station doorway, the boys were hit by a blast of lake-cooled air, forcing them to tightly button up their coats. It was now well past midnight, but the traffic and noise ensured the feel of a big city. The security guard gave them a strange look as they made the turn onto the pavement and started to walk.

"I can't believe we are actually in Chicago! How about we walk around six or seven blocks and just turn down where it looks interesting before coming back?" Adam's words were accompanied by the rising water vapour from his warm, moist breath.

After making a left turn down an adjacent road, the boys had walked only about two and a half blocks when they heard a voice behind them.

"Have you got any cigarettes?"

Initially surprised, the boys turned around to face a man standing only a couple of feet behind them.

"No, sorry. We don't smoke," replied Matt as he looked the man up and down, trying to assess whether the stranger was a threat or just an inquisitive passer-by. The man looked to be of mixed race, but determining what those races were eluded Matt.

Appearing to be in his mid-thirties, the man wore a long, light-coloured trench coat that covered a purple suit. His shoulder-length hair was very untidy and looked greasy and unwashed. His face had very sharp features, but there was something else that made it stand out, something strange. Matt suddenly realised what it was: the stranger had extremely long eyelashes.

Expecting him to move on after his denied request, the boys were surprised as the man made no effort to move and instead asked, "Have you got any money so I can buy some?"

Adam's reply was again meant to encourage the intruder to move on, but the man continued with his questions.

"What are your names?"

Instinctively, Matt answered. "He's Adam, and I'm Matt."

However, as soon as the words had left his mouth, Matt realised he had not made a wise decision.

"Adam and Matt, are you here by yourselves? Where are you going to?" The man's questions were starting to make them feel uncomfortable.

This time, Adam replied. "We're heading back to the train station; our friends are waiting for us and are probably wondering where we are."

Adam was aware his words sounded unconvincing; nevertheless, the boys turned around and started their trek back.

"I know a shortcut to the station; you can follow me."

"No, we're fine, thanks. We'll go back the way we came."

"I know somewhere you can sleep tonight if you're tired."

The man's comment was the last straw for the naive Matt and Adam. The situation had gone past being uncomfortable and was starting to get downright scary. Matt's logical mind told him there were two of them and only one of him; that, along with the fact they were probably stronger, meant they should have the upper hand if anything happened. Despite what his logical mind told him, there was something about this stranger that sent a shiver down his spine. As the boys increased their pace, they realised that they were probably a lot fitter, and should they choose to run, they could easily outrun their unwelcome guest. But somehow, they knew it wasn't the best thing to do. Just continuing to briskly move on and not respond to the man's continual questions was a far better plan.

It was with great relief that the station and its unfriendly, but now welcome, security guard appeared in sight.

Matt thought to himself – *This sort of thing would never happen in Mason.*

Police Chief Parker had certainly kept an eye on vagrants and other undesirables. Questionable people would be told to keep their time in Mason to a bare minimum. The police chief had a firm but fair policy, and in genuine cases, destitute vagrants would be offered a free meal, followed by a ride to the outskirts of town. A strong police presence ensured that Mason offered a safe, family-friendly environment for all its citizens. As for Chicago, well. . . if the man following them represented even just a small percentage of the local population, then living in Mason appeared to be a much better option.

Approaching the station entrance, the security guard recognised the boys who had left less than thirty minutes previously and allowed them access, but still without the slightest hint of a smile. Matt turned to check whether their unwelcome acquaintance was still following; to his relief, the stranger was nowhere to be seen.

They sat in the waiting room, their hearts still pounding. The events of the last hour had left the boys anxious and certainly not in any condition for having a good sleep. They knew the remainder of the night was going to be long.

As they boarded the train to Denver, they were excited to find their accommodation for the next eighteen hours was far superior to the previous train. The seats had good padding and were quite comfortable. In addition, the carriage had a different layout, with alternating seats facing forward and aft, resulting in separate areas that each contained a small table mounted under the window between the seats that faced each other. The table would hold little more than a couple of glasses. Although their assigned seats were the adjacent two on row six, when it became apparent that they would have no neighbours facing them, Matt moved across to the window seat at row five.

The boys watched Chicago slowly change from the city to suburbia. Yet, despite all there was to see outside, it was less than an hour before the rhythmic swaying of the passenger car combined with their lack of sleep induced them to drift off.

"What's wrong?" muttered Matt as he was awakened by Adam gently nudging him in the ribs.

"Nothing's wrong, but that girl over there has been staring at me and smiling." Adam nodded his head slightly towards row three on the other side of the carriage.

"What's she like?" enquired Matt.

"Come across and sit next to me, then you can see her. We can look at the map together so it's not obvious."

The girl, who was approximately their age, was sitting on the inboard seat facing towards them. Her curly, shoulder-length, dark-blonde hair was evenly parted in the middle, and her face was bubbly and full of life with the look of both innocence and sensuality. Although he was far from a fashion expert, the dark blue dress that she was wearing looked very expensive to Matt, and it complemented her large, light-blue eyes. Matt thought she was, indeed, pretty. She was not Christine, but very pretty nevertheless. After alternating his focus for a few minutes between the map and the girl, Matt returned to his seat.

"So, what do you think?" Adam whispered.

"She's very pretty. She was smiling at me, as well."

"Oh, was she?" Adam sounded disappointed.

"Probably only because I'm a friend of yours. It was you she saw first. Go talk to her."

Adam looked a bit sheepish. "What should I say?"

"I don't know. I'm not really the person to ask. I've had no experience sweet-talking girls. I guess just tell her your name, and if she likes you, she'll tell you hers."

Adam took a deep breath and summoned up his courage before getting up to make the small move forward in the carriage. He returned to his seat less than a minute later.

"How'd you get on?"

"Her name is Lyndy, and she's travelling with her family. But they've all gone to the dining car. Her dad is in the army."

"And what else did she say?"

"Nothing. It was obviously my turn to tell her about myself, but I got nervous and said I'd better get back to my friend. I think she likes me, though." Adam felt extremely disappointed with himself, but suddenly smiled as he had an idea. "Why don't you go up and say to her that your friend enjoyed talking to her and ask if she'd like to join us at our seats. When she's over here, you can help me out if I don't know what to say."

"I can't talk to her; I'd be more nervous than you were."

"Just pretend it's Jenny or Christine you're talking to."

"You could've done that."

"Well, I only just thought about it. So go on; do it for me."

This time, it was Matt who took the deep breath. He got up and took the few steps forward, then stopped to look at Lyndy, who was reading her book. She lifted her eyes to acknowledge his presence.

"Hello, I'm Matt."

"Hello, Matt."

These were the only two words she said before her gaze returned to the pages of her book. Matt now felt extremely uncomfortable. Should he disturb her and continue the conversation or retreat to his seat? The latter seamed the easiest option.

"Sorry, Adam – I failed." Matt sank sheepishly into his seat. The beautiful girl was clearly not interested in him. Matt's mind went back to Mason; why couldn't he talk to her like he was talking to Jenny or Christine? Suddenly, Matt had a eureka moment that filled him with excitement. What if Lyndy was keen on Adam, and the two of them got together. Then, he'd be free to return to Mason and pursue Christine once he'd finished his time on the military base with Max. The more Matt thought about it, the more it seemed like a win–win situation. Lyndy was very beautiful, and Adam would surely be proud to have her as his gal. In turn, Matt could finally have Christine all to himself.

"I know she really likes you and wasn't interested in talking to me. Why don't you go ask her to come over, and I promise to do my best to help you out if you're struggling with what to say. Go on; do it. You'll regret it if you don't."

Matt's words gave Adam all the encouragement he needed to attempt a second meeting. Adam was just about to get up when the door at the end of the carriage opened. A large man, a woman and a young boy walked in and made their way to where Lyndy was sitting. They were clearly her family. The young boy was around ten and was dressed smartly. The petite woman must have been in her late thirties or early forties; she looked quite elegant but was not smiling. The man looked quite scary. He must have been at least six foot five, with a solid build. His short haircut and square jaw only confirmed what his uniform had already told Adam – that he was in the army, and in a fight, you would definitely want him on your side. The man instructed Lyndy to move across to the window seat as he took her position, facing aft, while his wife and son placed themselves on the forward-facing seats directly across from them.

Once seated, the man suddenly looked up, noting that Adam had been staring at them. Realising that his daughter was the subject of Adam's infatuation, the man's neutral composure immediately changed to that of a protective father as he locked eyes with Adam. The man's stare was intimidating and prompted Adam to turn his head towards the window and Matt. Although he was now facing away, Adam could feel the man's intense stare piercing the air, right into his personal space.

Adam couldn't help himself, and he turned his head back to check, only to find himself once again locking eyes with the man. Lyndy's dad didn't say a word, but he didn't need to. His expression said everything: *Stay away from my daughter unless you want both your arms ripped out of their sockets and rammed up your butthole.* Adam quickly looked away before moving outboard to the window seat across from Matt, a location he chose to keep for the remainder of the trip.

Chapter 5

"I hope you had a good journey." Max had a warm smile as he extended his hand to shake Adam's and Matt's. It had been a long journey, and their progress on a map gave no justice to the actual distance covered.

A short taxi ride later, Max dropped the boys off at a motel with instructions to get a good night's sleep as he would be collecting them at eight o'clock the following morning for their trip north. But a good night's sleep was not on the boys' agenda. Max had to be kidding. Things were far too exciting to just go to sleep. They were in a new city in a new state; it had been their first time on a train, and tomorrow would see them on an aeroplane! They talked into the night about what they were leaving behind and what the future might hold. They also conjectured about what their jobs were actually going to involve, where they might be working and what their work colleagues might be like. They agreed that if the others were like Max, then it would be a nice work atmosphere.

With military precision, the knock on the front door occurred at exactly eight a.m. Outside, a car was waiting with its trunk wide open, ready for their bags. It was a beautiful spring morning, cold and crisp, and their breath created misty trails as they greeted Max. The thirty-minute drive to the airport was filled with anticipation as their first flying experience drew close, and their excitement increased as the airfield came into view. Until now, the vapour trails they could see of aircraft flying high above had been the closest that the boys had been to the pictures they'd seen in books. But now, as the big Chevy was given clearance through a security barrier, they were only a football field's length away from the West Coast Airways 727 parked alongside the terminal building. This, however, was not their plane.

Located far out on the other side of the airport was a plain, white Convair 440, completely devoid of any markings except for its registration number on the aft end of the fuselage. Matt, Adam and Max were the final three passengers to board, with the door closing firmly behind them. They made their way to their seats in the last row, allowing them to observe their fellow passengers: two equal groups of men – one group in uniforms and the other in dark suits. Both Matt and Adam felt a bit underdressed in their casual trousers and shirts. No one on the aircraft spoke but, rather, just sat still, staring blankly ahead. Several of their fellow passengers were holding briefcases on their laps, a couple of them with such an intensity it was as if their lives depended on it. The boys both had a feeling of slight unease, but the feeling was soon dissipated by a warm smile from Max.

After a brief stop at a remote airfield where four of their fellow passengers departed, the Convair was soon airborne again, making its way to Washington Lake Air Force Base. Several vehicles awaited the arrival of the aeroplane's occupants as it taxied to its arrival gate. The plane emptied quickly, and Matt, Adam and Max were the last to disembark. They were shown to a white Chevrolet van with tinted windows. Upon entering the van and taking their seats, it became apparent that the windows were not just tinted but completely blacked out. With the closing door came the realisation that they had no view outside in any direction.

"Don't worry, the military is just a bit secretive about some of their equipment, and remember, we're only civilians who will be working with them." Again, Max's explanation and smile had a soothing effect. The two-hour drive was an opportunity for the boys to ask lots of questions about their upcoming adventure. Max was able to answer most of them, informing them that they would first have long interviews and have to fill out a lot of forms. They would initially be assigned to another air-force base, where they were currently being driven, that was working on joint projects with the army. They would be living on the base, with all their meals provided, and they would be playing a lot of sports and getting lots of exercise while doctors monitored their performance. Their wages would also be banked into an account for them that would be available at the end of each six-month secondment. The thought of being paid to play sports and exercise just seemed too good to be true for two, naïve, teenage boys. A couple of judder bars and sharp turns preceded the van's final stop, when the doors opened to reveal that they were now inside a building.

"Follow me," ordered the air-force officer, who then pointed to their luggage. "Leave those in the van. They will be delivered to your living quarters."

A short walk led the trio to an office with two adjoining rooms, one of which Matt was led into, with Adam led into the other. Matt turned to Max, whose thumbs-up signal and big smile gave him the reassurance he needed. Several padded chairs and a wooden table stacked with a pile of papers greeted Matt as a voice sounded from behind.

"Please, take a seat. I'm Sergeant Benson, and we just need to get some formalities out of the way. Standard forms for privacy, security and safety."

One by one, without reading anything, Matt signed form after form as instructed by the sergeant. It could have been twenty or thirty signatures – Matt lost count. He was glad to see the last one, which upon completion was collected by the sergeant along with all the others and placed in a box. Then, the sergeant abruptly left with the box.

No sooner had he gone than he was replaced by an imposing officer whose big hand grabbed Matt's in a firm handshake.

"Matthew Brown, I'm Major Curtis, and this is Doctor Stoltz. Thank you for coming. I guess you have many questions."

Indeed, Matt did, but despite Major Curtis's opening line, there was no opportunity to ask anything over the next two and a quarter hours. The major and the doctor totally dominated the conversation, which turned into a series of questions that became increasingly more bizarre. It was only afterwards that Matt realised he had been subjected more to a psychological assessment than an interview. After a half-hour break that allowed a visit to an adjacent toilet, Matt was given a cup of coffee and a few sandwiches. Then, the interview resumed, this time with a Major Johnson and a man in a dark suit, introduced only as Cooper. A third man sat silently in the corner, taking notes. This man was not introduced to Matt. It had been a long day, and having had only a few hours' sleep the night before, about forty minutes into the second interview, Matt decided that he'd had enough. His sudden outburst regarding the stupidity of the questions had little, if any, effect on his interviewers. They simply let him have his say, then proceeded with the questioning. Matt had lost track of time and was aware that his answers were becoming more and more sarcastic as he tired, then suddenly, the major and

Cooper stood up, smiled and offered their hands in a friendly gesture.

"Thank you, Matthew. We've heard all that we need, and we welcome you to the project."

Matt was momentarily stunned and returned the handshake. "Thanks," he muttered weakly.

"I guess you're a bit hungry by now, so a driver will take you to the canteen and then back to your accommodation, where you'll find all the information that you'll need about your schedule."

The major's hand beckoned Matt's exit from the room. Matt instinctively looked around for any sign of either Adam or Max.

"Max said to say sorry he missed you, but he had to get back to Denver, and your friend is already at his accommodation. You'll be able to catch up with him later."

'Later', however, meant the following day. As much as he was longing to catch up with Adam and compare notes about their interviews, it was apparent that they wanted Matt to be rested, and he reassured himself that he would have time to spend with Adam the following day. The accommodation was certainly nothing to complain about. The bedroom was not large, with most of the space taken up by a big bed, which was the most comfortable that Matt had ever lain on. The apartment had a separate, small living area, one end of which contained a table with coffee-making facilities. The bathroom, while small, had a hot, high-pressure shower that made the day seem not so bad after all. After grabbing the schedule, Matt threw himself onto the bed. A quick scan of the schedule found that it gave very little away except the times that he would be collected each day, mealtimes and some of the physical activities that he would take part in. A note attached to the bottom informed him that he would get a phone call each morning exactly half an hour before he was due to be collected. Matt spotted the telephone and instinctively picked up the receiver. He thought that maybe he could sneak in a call to Christine in the next day or two. *Surely, they won't mind.* Not expecting there to be anyone on the other end, the ensuing "Hello? Base operator," startled him and he quickly replaced the receiver.

Matt realised that he must have had a good night's sleep, starting shortly after his head hit the pillow. There was a groggy awareness of the phone ringing for a few moments before he was roused enough from his deep sleep to answer it.

"You will be collected in half an hour."

The message was short and to the point. Matt had barely enough time to shower, dress and make a cup of coffee before the knock on his door.

"Good morning. Follow me, please." A hand gestured to a waiting Jeep, allowing Matt one last gulp of his half-drunk beverage. The ten-minute drive afforded a new clarity of the surroundings that Matt had not been able to appreciate the night before. His apartment was in one of about twenty buildings that were fully encircled by an imposing security fence. A uniformed guard opened the gate at a signal from the driver, allowing the Jeep to continue the drive along an unsealed road towards another much larger secured location that more resembled a military base. Once through the gate, the Jeep entered a building, drove down a ramp to the first underground level and stopped outside a doorway that framed the figure of Major Curtis.

It would be fair to say that while what Max had told Matt was not untrue, it was also not a fully fair representation of what life would really be like for Matt during his time at the base. Opportunities to spend time with Adam were limited, and they were never allowed to be by themselves. There would always be someone else around, and they had the distinct feeling that whatever they said was being listened to. Adam was staying at a separate compound within the main base, so there was actually very little chance to catch up outside of their organised activities. Matt was allowed only a few brief phone calls and was told in no uncertain terms that his calls were monitored, and any mention of what went on at the base would result in the call being terminated. A call to Christine in October brought the news that she and Julian had both been offered jobs in North Dakota, which gave her the opportunity to look after him. How he missed Mason and, in particular,

Christine... However, he knew that what he was doing was for the betterment of his life.

Despite the restrictions that life on base presented, things weren't all bad. Matt would often lie in bed and remind himself of what he had. There were certainly no complaints about the food, as he was fed extremely well with tasty, nourishing meals, and for someone who loved physical activity and sports, this place was heaven. Swimming and athletics were interspersed with regular medical check-ups and monitoring. Matt knew that he'd been asleep during some of the procedures, but he never knew for how long. It could have been two minutes or twenty-four hours, for there was no relevance to time. There were no clocks, and no one that he was in contact with ever wore a watch. Even the days of the week became a blur, but each day was much the same as the day before, so it didn't really matter. Life became a routine. Matt enjoyed the sports, eating well and sleeping well, and he was in good health. He had never felt so fit in his life, yet he couldn't wait for some of the promised trips away and, ultimately, for when the twelve months were up and he was free to collect his money and leave.

Heavy knocking on the door, not the phone ringing, woke him on the morning of 22 December 1966. It was a day that would change Matt's life forever. Still half-asleep, Matt slowly opened the door. He was greeted with the imposing sight of three large men in military police uniforms.

"What's going on?" he mumbled.

The sergeant stared blankly at Matt. "You have seven minutes to get dressed and collect all of your belongings. These men will assist you."

"What? Seven minutes? Are you joking? I've just woken up!"

The stare remained on the sergeant's face remained unchanged. "You now have six minutes and fifty seconds. May I suggest that you hurry?"

Barely dressed and with his possessions roughly thrown into two khaki rucksacks, Matt was driven at breakneck speed to the military facility that he had come to know as his second home. However, once inside the gates, the Jeep took a different route from the normal one and entered a building that he'd never been in before. Although it was still early in the morning, from the minute they entered the gate, Matt noted that everything was very different on this day. There were a lot of people around, all moving with a sense of urgency. Many trucks appeared to be in the process of being hastily loaded.

After ushering Matt into a reception area of the building, the sergeant departed, leaving the two remaining military guards to keep a watchful but expressionless eye on their charge. What was in reality less than five minutes seemed like an eternity before, finally, the door once again opened.

Two large men, both dressed in dark suits, entered, and one turned to the two guards. "You can leave us now. Thank you, gentlemen; we'll look after him from here."

There seemed to be a bit of hesitation on the part of the guards, prompting the man to walk to the door and hold it open. "Gentlemen!"

This time, the two guards complied. The unknown man closed the door behind them and then opened another door that led to an adjacent room. He indicated for Matt to walk in.

"Matthew, we need to have a little talk as to what has been happening. Firstly, though, I must stress that, at this point in time, I am probably the best friend you have in the world."

Matt's attention was drawn to the man as he spoke. He seemed friendly, and it appeared to a hopeful Matt that he was about to offer an explanation as to what was going on. Matt had, however, failed to notice that the second man had manoeuvred himself behind Matt. Suddenly, Matt felt movement as a large, strong hand held a cloth over his mouth and nose as another hand pushed his head forward. Matt noticed that the cloth was damp and had a strange smell. He tried to struggle free, but his struggle was short-lived and began losing intensity as Matt felt the sensation of sleepiness fill his head.

Matt's mind slowly began making sense of his surroundings. He was lying on a bed in a windowless room. The thickly painted, cream-coloured brick wall gave the sense of being in a sterile environment, perhaps a medical facility. It was a potential scenario that was reinforced as Matt slowly raised his head and turned to see a masculine-looking, female nurse who correspondingly called out in an equally masculine voice, "He's awake now."

Still semi-groggy, Matt was greeted by a man entering the room. Matt had never met the man before, but the man knew him.

"Good morning, Matthew. I'm sorry about the rude way that we got you here. I know this is going to be hard to believe, but it was for your own good. As you've probably gathered, a few things have changed for us."

"So, what is happening? Why am I here, and who are you?"

"That's not important, Matthew. What is important is that you've helped your country, and now it's time for your country to repay its debt to you."

"I'm sorry, but I don't understand. Am I in some kind of trouble?"

"No, not at all! Quite the contrary. Things have. . . well – shall I say, wound down a little at the base, and unfortunately, we must let you go. But don't worry; Uncle Sam is going to look after you. We've organised a fantastic new life for you—a place to live, a good job, and a nice financial nest egg to get your new life started;

in fact, everything you will need for a successful beginning to your wonderful new life, including a new identity. Rest assured, you will be well looked after, but it will require your full cooperation."

"A new identity?!" Matt could not conceal the shock that suddenly gripped him.

"Yes, a new identity, complete with a new name and a new family history. From today, your previous life, including your time at the base, never existed. It will mean you will not be able to contact anybody you knew prior to this exact moment. We will give you a completely new past, with all the documentation you need to support it. Life is all about looking forward and not back; it will be a totally new life, but I promise you, it will be a good life. You're a very lucky man to be given this opportunity. I will need to take all your documents, including your bank book, but don't be concerned – you will definitely not be financially disadvantaged."

Matt realised that he was shaking. "Thanks, but no thanks. I don't want to sound ungrateful, but I can't give up my past. If the project has finished, then I will just leave, and I won't say anything to anybody about my time here."

The man looked at Matt for what seemed like an eternity. "John – by the way, your new name is John – you don't seem to understand that you do not have a choice. Either way, from this day on, you have a new life, and that life has already started. . . John."

"But. . . but I can't just give up my past, my friends and Adam! What has happened to him? I want to know. I have my rights!"

"You signed away your rights when you arrived here, John. You should have read what you were signing. You do not need to be concerned about Adam; we'll be looking after him as well. But listen carefully – Adam is no longer a part of your life, be it past, present or future. This is really not a bad situation for you, because if you cooperate with our terms and requirements, then you will be well looked after and you'll have a good life. There will be plenty of new friends in the future.

"However, should you choose not to fully cooperate, then I'm afraid that, without exception, we won't be able to let you leave, and you will never see anything outside of a room just like this, because you will be detained at a secure location for the rest of your natural life. So, John, as I see it, the choice is obvious. But you're the one who has to make that decision. Think very carefully about everything that I have just said. I am only giving you one minute to tell me what your answer is going to be."

Chapter 6

November 1989

Dobson's Hardware in Pine Ridge was a successful business and, without a doubt, the largest hardware supplier in the county. Employing ten full and part-time staff, the business had been founded twenty-two years earlier on humble beginnings by an enthusiastic twenty-year-old John Dobson. John had been brought up by his grandfather in rural California, and from a young age, he'd had the values of hard work, honesty and customer service instilled into him. John had inherited his grandfather's house, and he'd used the money to purchase a small hardware and general-supply store that had been put up for sale by its elderly owners. Now, many years of hard work later, John, his wife Nancy and the store were pillars of the local community.

A true story? No, not the bit about the grandfather and John's boyhood. Nobody in Pine Ridge, not even Nancy, knew the real story of the first eighteen years of John's life. The real financier of John's original purchase was not his grandfather but, rather, a nameless government department that seemed keen to get John's life off to a good start, a government department that also pulled out all the stops in creating a new identity for the old Matt Brown before relocating him to Pine Ridge as John Dobson, complete with a new birth certificate that saw him gaining a whole year in age. During the healing time for the appearance-altering cosmetic surgery, John was given private tutoring in business skills, financial investing and people management, all of which would become very useful as John increased the size of his business tenfold to become what it was today.

Immediately upon taking possession of the business, John had even been given the services of Marty McDonald, a businessman posing as an assistant. Marty's job was to help John run the store for the first six months. Firstly, it was to help a naive young man find his feet in his new environment, and secondly, it gave John the time to find a full-time assistant. During those first six months, John became good friends with Marty and relied heavily on his advice, never more so than when it came to selecting and employing a full-time assistant. John would never have picked Nancy if it had not been for Marty's influence, for as John saw it, a woman just did not work in a hardware store. However, the decision to hire her was one that he was glad he'd made. Nancy was a hard worker; she was intelligent and business minded. Six years his senior, Nancy was also very beautiful, a fact not missed by John. A little more than a year after they had met, John married the girl who had started as an assistant but had now become a business and life partner.

Everything in life has a price, and for John, it was keeping his end of a bargain. This meant no contact with anybody or anything from his previous life, something that did become slightly easier over time. There were other requirements of the agreement, including his regular monthly medical check-ups. These were not just any check-up with any doctor, but prearranged appointments for what were intensive medical exams—always with the same specific doctor. John had been informed that he was never to visit any regular doctor or medical facility. In fact, if he was unwell or it was an emergency, he was instructed to dial a special phone number from any phone at any time. However, the truth of the matter was that John enjoyed particularly good health over the years, never getting sick and only suffering from the odd cuts or minor injuries consistent with his job. To John, the irony of the compulsory doctor's visits was that it was only after them that he felt unwell. John had always put this down to the quantity of blood the doctor took from him.

Life for John and Nancy was pleasant. They had a nice house, a successful business, good customers and good friends. However, the one thing that remained missing was the completion of their family with children. As Nancy was unable to conceive, it was not a subject that she seemed keen to talk about, but when prompted by John, she would simply say that it didn't bother her, and she would never pursue it further with her doctor. John knew, however, that inside, she was upset and longed to become pregnant, and his suspicions were reinforced every time he saw her with young children, especially little girls.

Nancy's parents had moved to Pine Ridge about a year after she and John were married. It was Nancy's idea to have her parents close by; she'd often talked with John about it after their marriage. John was quite receptive to the idea, and when they finally agreed, he was actually quite excited. John had got on well with them from the first time that he'd met them, and as the years passed, he grew to love Bill and Judith like parents, for they had become the parents John had never had. Sometimes, when helping Judith with baking, he would sift the flour or mix in the chocolate chips, and he'd feel just like a seven-year-old boy helping his mum. John also enjoyed the quality time he spent with Nancy's father. Nancy's older brother, Kenney, had been killed a few years earlier during a training accident in the navy, something the family never talked much about. But they were clearly still grieving over the tragedy. Consequently, just as Bill had become a substitute father, John had become a substitute son.

Often, on their days spent together, John and Bill would spend many hours fishing and solving the world's problems. Bill was a man of seemingly unbounded knowledge; whatever the subject John initiated, Bill more than held his own in the conversation, supporting his comments with facts and details on the subject that often left John dumbfounded. There was, however, one subject for which Bill had a particular passion – politics.

Neither a Democrat nor Republican, Bill would share with John his ideas for what he saw as a prosperous and politically harmonised United States that was positioned between the extremes of capitalism and socialism: a place where every person, regardless of race, age or creed, would have access to affordable medical resources and a minimum standard of living that would be the envy of people from many other parts of the world. America would be a country where every person who wanted to could pursue the dream of achieving wealth through hard work and entrepreneurship without been crippled by a system and its taxes that favoured big corporations over small business owners. In Bill's utopian concept, every person who lived within her borders could be proud to be an American and would step forward without hesitation to defend her and what she stood for.

John had raised the question numerous times with Bill why, with all his knowledge, he had never entered politics.

Bill's answer was always the same: "John, I was not made for politics, and politics was not made for me."

It was a response that often left John puzzled, considering Bill's passion for the subject, until one hot

Sunday afternoon in July 1982 when the fish were just not biting.

As the boat gently rocked back and forth, Bill removed a small bottle of whisky and two glasses from his backpack. The glasses were soon half-filled with the amber liquid as Bill proposed a toast. "To all the smart fish in this river that realise taking the bait will be their undoing."

John acknowledged the toast. "To the smart fish."

"Perhaps those fish are smarter than us so-called clever humans who so easily take bait."

"I'm not quite sure what you mean, Bill," John replied.

"You have asked me a few times why I never went into politics. Do you really think I'm the only person with the dreams that I have? My ideas are not strange, and they're not new. There are many good men and women who would like to see the country a better place for all. Many good people enter politics wanting to change the world for the better, only to realise the system can never be beaten. They soon find out that the only way to get ahead is to conform to a system that corrupts, and I would not be true to myself or my beliefs if I had to change."

"I know the system isn't perfect, Bill, but surely we are much better off than many other countries. We have the freedom to vote and elect our political representatives."

"That is somewhat true, but not totally. Presidents are groomed and their policies drafted long before they ever reach the gates of the White House. They may be elected, but all elections are steered in a certain direction. Before the constitution was even drafted, the puppeteers of this world were preparing to guide the future of the United States, just like they'd guided Europe for the last millennium."

Bill's conversation progressed to Ronald Reagan and what he had in common with the thirty-nine preceding presidents. Most of what Bill said, John had heard before in various forms, but this time, Bill's speech was filled with emotion that somehow allowed John to fully comprehend what he was trying to say. Finally, Bill's passion for the things that he could not change all now made sense. Nine words finished the subject of the conversation: "And that, John, is why I never entered politics."

John hoped that this poignant moment might also be the opportunity that Bill would share more about the two things that he knew he'd been excluded from—firstly, the full story of what had actually happened to Kenney and his accident in the navy.

Secondly, there was the family secret – one that despite its obvious existence, the family chose to keep hidden in the dark shadows of denial. Apart from her brother's death, something else had happened to Nancy's family, something so traumatic that despite the status he had gained in the family, John was not privy to.

To his great disappointment, this would not be the occasion of his inclusion.

John had often tried to approach the subject with his wife, but Nancy had an amazing ability to change a conversation around to a completely different subject when she needed to. John felt a little hurt by this exclusion, but he would remind himself that he also had his own secrets, and his were surely far bigger than theirs could ever be, so he conceded his exclusion from theirs. When Nancy's parents died in 1986 and 1987, John was just upset as Nancy. Their deaths left a huge gap in their lives.

Although John was quite content with his new life, on 31 December 1989, as they celebrated New Year's Eve with some friends, reality hit home. There was only one more year before the planned reunion with his four friends. He did not realise it at the time, but it was at that point that the rest of his life changed. In the beginning, twenty-five years had seemed such a long time away, but now that the remaining period could be measured in months, the time left gave him a sense of urgency. The countdown was on.

1990 became a stressful time for John. Many nights, he lay in bed, unable to sleep as conflicting thoughts battled to take control of his mind. In one camp were the thoughts that reminded him of the threatened consequences of contacting anybody from his past. Lying in bed with Nancy cuddled up to him, he knew how much she loved him and how much he had to lose if the authorities, or whoever they were, ever found he'd broken that agreement.

In the other camp were the thoughts of the four friends he'd grown up with. What was Adam doing now? Was he still alive? Did he also now have a new identity? Or was he allowed to return to his old life? All John had to go on was when he'd been told at the base: "You do not need to be concerned about Adam; we'll be looking after him as well."

Either way, was he married? Did he have children? So many questions bounced around in John's mind. What about Julian? Was life any better for him than before? Had he grown out of his extreme shyness? Had he found a woman to share his life with? John could see Julian with a wife, someone who looked at what people were like on the inside. He could also see her as a very homely sort of person. His thoughts turned to Jenny: Julian's number-one protector. Would she make the reunion? How on earth would she explain to Jean-Michel a visit home to America by herself? But then again, was she still married to her soft-spoken French husband, or did she separate to find someone who was more like herself? Regardless of her situation, she would probably have several children. But how many? Maybe it would be too hard for her to come back to America. But then again, she was one of the most dependable people that Matt had ever met. Surely, if anybody would be there, it would be Jenny.

Last, but not least, Christine – the beautiful Christine and her big blue eyes. John loved Nancy dearly, but if he was honest with himself, there were far too many times that while he was making love to Nancy, he would close his eyes and it would be Christine he would see underneath him, and it would be her and not Nancy who was moaning. Even after all this time, it was still Christine who truly made his heart race, and losing contact with her was the hardest part of his new life. John knew a woman like Christine could have had her choice of men; she had probably married a surgeon and lived in a big house with a couple of beautiful children and pedigree dogs running around. If that were the case, and he could see she loved her husband and her life, then maybe he could get her out of his mind. But at the same time, John was filled with both guilt and excitement at the thought that Christine's husband may have died or they may have gotten divorced, leaving Christine lonely and in need of the affection that he was willing to offer her.

As the year progressed, John's restless nights increased in intensity. He would often wake up drenched in a cold sweat. It felt like a civil war was taking place in John's mind, with one side saying *go*, and the other side saying *stay*. The worst thing was that there were valid arguments for both sides, and John felt ripped right down the middle. As his brain struggled to deal with the conflicting emotions, John wished that he had someone he could confide in, someone who could see his predicament from an unbiased angle. With irony having it that Nancy, his wife and the closest person in his life, was now the last person he could confide in, an understanding brother or sister would have been a godsend.

Maybe, out there somewhere in the world, he did have siblings, maybe even parents who were still alive, but the reality was that it didn't really matter, for it was so long ago that any leads would be cold. And worse still, any attempt to track them down would only expose his real history. John had gone as far as getting the names of several counsellors from the local phone book; the initiating phone calls, however, were never made. This was clearly something he had to sort out all by himself.

One Friday in September, John heard the song by The Clash, "Should I Stay, or Should I Go?" playing on his car radio. Finding himself turning up the volume and singing along, John felt the song was almost written for him, and he couldn't help but wonder if the writer of the lyrics had been going through the same internal conflict as he was when they wrote the words.

John was a very logical man, and logic quite simply said, "Don't go; leave it in the past!" He was well aware of the consequences of not fulfilling his end of the agreement, but unfortunately for him, it was not only his logical side that he was dealing with. His emotions were quite clearly going to play a big part in his final decision. Sometimes, when he was alone and sure nobody could hear, he would ask himself, out loud, how he would feel if everybody except himself turned up. Could he live with himself afterwards, knowing that might have happened? What about if only Christine made it, and she was alone, wandering around looking for her friends? It could be his opportunity to see her again, just the two of them, and who knows what might happen. Or the worst possible scenario, what if it were only Adam and Christine who made the reunion, and as a result, they hooked up that night and Adam got what John had always wanted? Could he accept that possibility? No, he could not! It was this one particular thought that was just too unbearable, and the one that finally sealed his fate, for despite his better judgement, he knew that he must go. He would not be able to live with himself if he didn't.

However, it would not be until the end of November before he summoned up the courage to tell Nancy his well-prepared story.

John knew his reason for being away on New Year's Eve had to be convincing. After all, they had always celebrated with friends, and nobody, not even his wife, could find out the real place he intended to be. After much deliberation, his story went along the lines that he had been contacted by an old, high-school buddy from his football team who was planning a men-only reunion over the New Year in California. It was a story he planned not to relay to any of his staff or friends unless absolutely necessary and only much closer to the time.

Nancy was a quietly determined person. She normally got her own way, but never through anger or a raised voice; quite the opposite. In fact, John had never heard Nancy raise her voice once, so he was totally floored in disbelief at her reaction when he finally summoned up the courage to tell her about his planned trip.

"No, no, no... you will not be going! You just can't, and you won't. I will leave you if you do."

What followed was a solid, two-minute outburst that offered no reason for the forcefulness of her reaction, just a clear understanding that this was not going to happen under any circumstances. It was only after reassurance from John that he would not be going that she finally calmed down. However, it was a reassurance that was continually asked for and consequently given over the following four weeks.

Nancy's reaction that day was another complication in the thoughts in John's tormented mind. Initially, he reversed his decision to go, and at first, it brought some relief. But slowly, as the final weeks passed, he knew that he just could not live with himself if he did not fulfil his part of the long-standing pact. The only difference now was that he would not tell anybody, including Nancy, about going away; he would make his escape quietly and with the utmost secrecy.

His day at work on Saturday December 29 was going to be the longest in his life. That morning, as he showered, John went over his plans for the day. In the early afternoon, he would say that he was going to see some customers, but instead, he would drive due east on the start of his long journey. A couple of changes of clothes in the trunk should see him through a few days. He would use money that he had been quietly putting aside over the last year, as paying in cash would not leave a credit card trail and clues to his intended destination.

As far as rest during the long journey, he would sleep in the car as needed and would find a motel when he got to Mason. If he got desperate for a good sleep, there was always the option to find a motel for a few hours, but not on the first night. He would drive straight through to get a good head start, just in case Nancy decided to try to stop him once she realised he was gone. The one thing he believed was in his favour was that Nancy should be thinking that his journey was taking him southwest towards California rather than east towards Ohio.

John's story was initially quite convincing as the customer that he was supposed to be going to see did actually owe them money, but as he walked out of the store, John suddenly had a gut-wrenching feeling that he would never see any of his staff again. He was initially tempted to say goodbye to each and every one of them, especially Bob, his most trusted employee, who had worked for John for the last seventeen years. But knowing that it would only arouse suspicion, his goodbye consisted of "I'll be back in an hour or two" to a busy Nancy, who seemed quite relaxed about his afternoon outing.

Last-minute fear and guilt caused his heart to suddenly race as thoughts of the worst-case scenario entered his head. What if he was the only one to turn up, and it was a complete waste of time? After all, it was twenty-five years ago, and they would all have new lives. Not everybody lives in the past. Additionally, what if because of this non-event he lost Nancy, his home, his business, his staff and friends?

John started shaking as he walked towards the car, and by the time he was inside and had the key in the ignition, his right foot was moving uncontrollably with nerves. John paused for a moment, taking in a deep breath. His stomach had been churning all morning. This was the final and deciding battle of the civil war that had been playing out in his mind for the last twelve months. After all this time, this was it, decision time, for whatever he decided to do. There would be no going back. He could be driving away from everything that he had, but he knew inside that, above all else, it would be his only opportunity to ever see Christine and his friends again.

John finally turned the key, allowing the big Dodge to fire up. As the car idled, John suddenly had a thought. *If Adam had found himself in the same scenario, living with a new identity, then would he also have a wife who did not know about the first eighteen years of his life? Perhaps somewhere in the country, Adam could be sitting in a car at that very same moment, also weighing up the consequences of his actions.* Somehow, the thought made John feel not so alone and separated from the rest of the world.

Taking a big breath, he put the car into gear and told himself out loud,

"Go, go, go! Just do it!"

The car moved forward out of the parking area onto the road with a slight squeal from the rear tyres. Nerves were now joined by a feeling of relief. Be it right or wrong, he had finally made the decision.

Chapter 7

John swallowed with a dry throat as he drove past the sign informing him that he was leaving Pine Ridge. It was probably the realisation that, after all this time of indecision, he was now finally committed and there was no going back. Anything that happened as a result was now beyond his control and would be decided by others. After a year of internal torment, this thought generated a feeling of relief.

The main road had turned into an expressway, which had, in turn, become a freeway, allowing the miles to disappear a lot quicker. John glanced at his speedometer. Months of planning had allowed him to calculate an average speed that would be required for the journey, one that was achievable and a compromise between getting there safely and getting there quickly. The Dodge's large motor yearned to be let loose, and as tempting as it was to unleash its three hundred and twenty-five ponies, John was aware that a speeding vehicle could attract the attention of the police, or worse still, increase his chances of having an accident, which could see him not only missing his rendezvous but possibly waking up in a hospital bed with Nancy looking over him. He could lose her forever and not even be able to attend the reunion as compensation. No, he would keep to a safe speed.

It was not long into John's journey before the light had quickly progressed through dusk to dark, bringing with it a windy chill. The threat of heavy snow or even a blizzard was always a possibility. A light dusting of white already covered the surrounding farmland as the altitude of the terrain increased. The Dodge's heater was set to the warmest possible selection and was doing its best; however, John thought a few extra degrees would make the long drive just that bit more bearable. He struggled with the radio, trying to locate another station that was close enough to get tuned in. Not having much luck, he turned to his collection of favourite cassettes that were placed in a container under the passenger seat. It wasn't long before Elton John and the Doobie Brothers had joined him on his journey.

The miles and hours ticked by as John repeatedly spoke out the opening line that he would say to Christine, the same line that he was repeating as he pulled in to make his first gas stop. Stepping from the warm car, John realised just how cold it had become. The time spent waiting for the tank to fill allowed him to retrieve some of the items he'd previously placed in the trunk, including a scarf, a hat, a heavy duty coat and two thermoses of once-hot but now only lukewarm strong and sweet coffee. John was going to make sure that all his purchases over the next few days were cash only. Perhaps he was paranoid, but having a credit card trail did not seem like a good idea. So after a cash payment to the petrol station and with a cup of coffee in John's belly, the Dodge's wheels once again began to eat up the miles.

    The clock on his dashboard clicked over to the early hours of Sunday. John had kept his rest options open; he knew rest was important, but at this point, he just wanted to get Pine Ridge as far behind him as he could. After all, the less time he slept on the way gave him more time to rest when he got to Mason. Eventually, sleep beckoned, and indeed, a motel bed would be so comfortable. But not tonight; he was still too close to home. A quiet lay-by adjacent to a scenic viewpoint seemed too much of a good opportunity to pass up for a few hours of much-needed rest. A couple of thick blankets and a pillow that were also retrieved from the trunk during his petrol stop would be John's only comfort on this part of his journey. With the engine off, it didn't take long for the interior of the car to cool to the point that even the two blankets struggled to retain his body heat at a comfortable level, so a refreshing sleep was not possible. It was more like a rest interspersed with periods of pre-sleep semi-consciousness. Keeping the engine running for heat was an option that crossed John's mind, but somehow it just didn't seem the right option to take, so an hour and a half of almost sleep would have to get him through to the following night, when he would find a motel for a few hours of proper sleep.

John had been on the road only for a little more than two hours after his rest when his headlights picked up movement in the distance. His bloodshot eyes could have easily missed the person had they not moved into his path with frantically waving hands. The Dodge came to a stop, with its interior instantly cooling as John powered down the window.

The woman looked at John for a moment before speaking. "Please, can I get into your car? I'm so cold."

Closing the window and unlocking the door, John allowed the woman to get into the passenger's seat. She was shivering uncontrollably, which prompted John to reach into the back seat and pass her the two blankets that had been his companions hours earlier. His enquiry if she was okay was met with a strange response.

"Thank God you're not a weirdo!"

"I am definitely not a weirdo; I've been called all sorts of things, but never a weirdo, not even by my wife!"

"No, seriously, I would never get into a stranger's car. I've never hitchhiked or anything like that. My dad used to say, 'Lana, never, never, never get into a stranger's car,' but my engine started spluttering a few miles back. Then there was a loud bang, and the car violently stopped. I tried to start it again, but it's totally dead, and there was a burning electrical smell, so I turned the key off and took it out."

She gestured to the grey Toyota sedan parked at an angle a few feet off the side of the road.

"I've been here about an hour, and I'm absolutely frozen to the bone. You're the first car that has passed. I had to flag you down, and I was praying that you weren't some sort of weird person; you hear so many horror stories."

"I think most people are okay. We always hear about the few bad events that happen but never the tens of thousands of good things."

"I like your attitude! You're definitely okay, thank God for that. I'm Lana Godfery." She held out her cold hand, and John shook it as he introduced himself.

"I'm John; I mean Hank."

Caught off guard, John realised that he should never have said his real name, and now changing it for another had aroused suspicion.

"So then, is it John or Hank?" Lana looked a little bit concerned about John's introduction.

"Oh, sorry. John Hankton, so it's John, but some people call me Hank." John's quick thinking made him feel better, and it also helped Lana feel more secure.

"Can I call you John, or do you prefer to be called Hank?"

"John will be fine. Should I drop you in the next town that has a garage so you can get your car towed?"

"To be honest, John, I think it's something major. And considering the car is so full of rust, I'm quite sure it's not worth spending money on. I live with my brother and sister-in-law, who I'll call later. Bob has a vehicle trailer, so I'm sure he can organise either getting it back home or to the scrap yard. But even if there was a phone, I won't call them at four thirty in the morning. What I really need is a ride east. I'm more than happy to pay my fair share of the gas."

"Where are you heading to?"

"Ohio, to meet some old friends."

"Ohio! Where about in Ohio?"

"Just outside of Dayton. If I can get to Dayton, my friends can pick me up from there."

John felt a sigh of relief flow through his body. He instinctively knew this lady was neither Christine nor Jenny, but when she said Ohio to meet some friends, there was a brief moment of doubt. After all, what were the odds? John knew he couldn't leave Lana on the side of the road in the freezing cold, and one of his route options took him through Dayton. She seemed like a nice person, and having a travelling companion to talk to would be nice. However, the situation also presented a major issue given that John's journey would no longer have the level of secrecy that it once did as Lana would know who he was and what direction he was travelling. But then again, she already knew both of those things! John realised he had nothing to lose by taking her along, and after all, he could always give her some misinformation just in case.

"I'm actually heading to New York State. I have a friend just outside of Buffalo, so it really is no big deal to go via Dayton."

John felt bad about telling Lana a lie about not only his family name but also his destination. But he knew it was a necessity, and it paled in comparison to what he'd told, or more correctly, not told, Nancy.

"Oh my God, that is an amazing stroke of good luck on my part! I would really appreciate the ride, and I will certainly do my bit with the fuel. I just need to get my bags out of the boot of my car."

Lana proved to be a very talkative travelling companion, and it wasn't long before John knew her complete life story. She was forty-one, divorced after a long restrictive marriage and had two daughters, nineteen and twenty-one, who shared an apartment in Denver. She now lived with her older brother, Bob, and his wife, Tammy, who unlike Lana, apparently had plenty of money. Lana was the younger, poor sister whose job at the local mall didn't allow for an extravagant lifestyle. She worked long hours and had been saving hard for a new car. During her wait for help, she had decided she didn't want to waste any of her savings repairing her old Toyota and would be happy just to walk away from it if necessary. Lana had been travelling to meet her lifelong friend Libby Patterson at her home outside Dayton so they could celebrate New Year's Eve together. Libby had recently been divorced herself and was living with her sister Joy. Their New

Year's get-together was to toast and celebrate the positive change of direction in both their lives and the new start that the upcoming year promised to bring.

After a stop for breakfast, fuel and that all-important call to Bob, they were back on the road. The conversation had unfortunately turned to John's life, including questions about his friend in Buffalo and why John's wife was not travelling with him. Quick thinking thankfully meant believable replies as John tried to keep his life story brief. A collection of half-truths helped to ease the guilt of the lies that were necessary to protect his true life history.

Time turned towards the past as the miles continued to tick over on John's odometer. Brief stops for petrol, lunch, coffee and toilet breaks broke the monotony of the endless roads. Lana had dozed off a few times, but for John, an hour and a half stop for a quick sleep just after midday had kept his mind just to the right side of sanity. Now, as Sunday afternoon progressed, nineteen of the last twenty-five hours had been spent behind the wheel, and it was beginning to take its toll. John knew he would need to find a place to rest properly. It was, however, Lana who brought up the subject.

"I should have said something before, but I didn't want this to sound wrong and for you to get the wrong idea, but the last time I made this trip, I stopped at a motel called the Triple M. It was recommended to me because they claim to have the most comfortable beds in the whole state, and from my experience last time, that's probably a fair claim. I afforded the luxury of booking a room for my trip east. There's an intersection further up with a road that leads to a town called Benson; we'd need to turn off there. The room is booked and paid for, so would you want to stop there? One thing, though, because you literally rescued the damsel in distress and you're doing the driving, you should have the bed, and I'll sleep on the sofa."

"That seems like a very good idea, but I'm quite happy to sleep on the sofa. After all, up till now, I've only slept in the car, so even a sofa is a definite improvement."

The Triple M Motel provided just what John needed: a properly nourishing dinner, a hot shower and a warm, quiet room. The bed resembled the deck of an aircraft carrier with the comfort to sooth any aching joint. The sofa, however, left a bit to be desired. It wasn't a size or shape to lie on comfortably, regardless of any contorted body position, leaving John with the inevitable decision to sleep on the floor. But Lana was having no part of that.

"There is no way I'm sleeping on the bed while you sleep on the floor! The bed is big enough so that if you stay on your side and I stay on this side, we won't disturb each other. And we can both get a good night's sleep. Half of this bed is bigger than my normal bed, anyway."

John agreed that it made perfect sense. He might have an attractive woman getting into the same bed as he was, but there was currently only one woman on his mind, and – who knew – maybe tomorrow he might be getting into bed with her. John knew he would sleep well, probably far too well. According to his calculations, he was well on schedule but he still had another eight to nine hours of driving to do, and he didn't want to arrive in Mason too late in the day. After conferring with Lana, who was under the impression that John still had over twelve hours left to drive to Buffalo, John set the bedside clock radio alarm for three fifteen a.m. That would allow for a four a.m. departure.

As soon as his body sank into the caressing, upper layers of the mattress, John could see how the motel was justified in making their claim to fame. The mattress was perfectly body moulding, but just firm enough to support the body's weight. Lying on the extreme side of the bed, John looked up as Lana exited the bathroom and made her way to her side. She was wearing nothing but a pair of black panties. She certainly wasn't flaunting her body, but then again, she certainly wasn't being shy about it, either. For Lana, it was really just a matter of fact that she wore only her underwear when sleeping, whether she was alone at home or sharing a large bed with a travelling companion.

Lana gave a quick, "Goodnight, John," before turning around to face the other direction.

Turning off the bedside lamp, John collected his thoughts. Was her topless walk from the bathroom to the bed the green light for him to roll across and pay her a visit? Would his advances be something that she was expecting of him, or would any action, no matter how small, be breaking the trust he'd gained and upset his newfound friendship? Was the fact that Lana was clad only in her panties any different to the fact that he wore just his underpants to bed? John had never been in such a situation before. There had only ever been two women in his life, and he'd slept with only one of them. There were currently enough complications in his life without adding Lana to the list, so it was with great relief that he realised Lana had already fallen fast asleep.

John asked himself what would he have done if Lana had said, 'Are you not going to give me a goodnight kiss then?' He realised that he didn't have the answer, but one thing he did know was that if a similar situation presented itself the next night and it was Christine on the other side of the bed, there would be no way he would be turning her down.

As he felt himself winding down, John's thoughts turned fully to Christine; thoughts that inevitably aroused him. His mind went through some of the possible scenarios. What if it were only the two of them who turned up? What if there weren't a lot of accommodations available and they had to share a room or a bed; would she be as beautiful as he remembered? Would she let him caress her back or even kiss her? Would she . . . the more John thought about Christine, the more aroused he became. Sleep, or to be precise, the lack thereof, soon got the better of him and his thoughts.

The tune from the bedside clock-radio gently brought John out of a deep sleep; the song was mellow and soothing, perhaps too soothing, as he could have remained there almost indefinitely. The dream that he had awoken from was fading fast, and John's brain physically hurt as he desperately tried to remember its content. Only a few parts remained clear, but he knew it involved Christine, and it was definitely a very pleasant dream.

As the gentle tones of George Benson issued from the clock radio and serenaded his half-conscious mind, John's attention was drawn to the fact that the woman sleeping next to him was neither Nancy nor Christine. It was his newfound friend, Lana. Somehow, during the night, the two weary travellers had migrated towards the centre of the bed. Now, John was lying on his stomach with his head turned away from Lana, his right arm folded up, with his hand under the pillow. His left arm, however, was down by his side, and it was what Lana was cuddled up close against. To his horror, John suddenly realised that his left hand was in quite a compromising position against her body.

"Oh, my God, I'm so sorry!" John's comment completed Lana's awakening from her deep sleep. It also made her realise where in the bed she'd been sleeping. "It's okay, nothing happened," John soothed, jumping out of the bed. Clad only in his underpants, he was even more horrified when he became aware that his thoughts of Christine had left him visibly aroused. "Um, I'll jump in the shower first. I won't be long," he mumbled, embarrassed, almost tripping over his clothes that were draped on the chair next to the bed. *Oh my God, she's going to think I was getting worked up over her. But I can't tell her it was actually Christine.*

A hot shower and a quick strong coffee brought them both to a point where they could hit the road again. Lana could have slept for a couple more hours, but John was a man on a mission, and this mission had a tight schedule. John also knew that Lana could always catch a few more hours' sleep as he drove.

Little was said about their sleeping arrangements the night before during their remaining hours together. Lana kept the conversation going on a wide variety of subjects. She may not have travelled much, but she was well informed about world events, history and other cultures, to name just a few things.

Robinson's Mall in Dayton was the end of Lana's journey. A phone call from a pay phone confirmed that her friend and her friend's sister would collect her from there. A handshake, long hug and kiss on the cheek signalled the departure of John's new friend. As he watched Lana's waving hand, John realised he would deeply miss her chirpy personality. Had it been any other situation, it would have been a lot worse. In fact, another time, another place, or another life. . . who knows? Things could have been very different. As Lana disappeared into the distance, John was comforted knowing that thoughts of Lana would soon be replaced by thoughts of what the next twenty-four hours held. After all, his destination and ultimately seeing Christine again were now only a few hours' drive away.

Welcome to Mason. It was just three simple words written in white letters on a green road sign, but it was enough to make John Dobson's car come to a complete stop. He jumped out of the car and slowly raised a clenched fist into the air. "Yes!" Congratulating himself, he took a deep breath of fresh country air, and how sweet it smelled.

John was filled with emotions. He wanted to dance, shout, sing and cry all at the same time, but he did none of these. Instead, as a tear rolled down his left cheek, he slowly got back into his car contemplating the reality of the situation for a few moments. Yes, he was finally back, and yes, it had taken twenty-five years, but it now seemed like only the other week that the bus had left.

Closing his eyes for a moment was a perfect opportunity for the now-weary traveller to catch his breath and collect his thoughts. Of all the smile-inducing memories that bombarded his mind, there was one in particular that stood out. It was an event between the pact being made and Jenny's departure. It had taken place in either late January or early February, and although he wasn't sure of the exact date, the picture had been visibly etched into his memory.

As a resident of the orphanage, going out to the movies was a very rare treat. But on this occasion, Jenny's employer had given her five tickets to see *Doctor Zhivago*, a movie that only she and Christine seemed to enjoy. Walking back under the light of the full moon gave an opportunity for the girls to explain the deeper meaning of a movie that did not contain shootouts with gangsters or ensuing car chases.

It was the same full moon that silhouetted the orphanage with an eerie, blue glow through the light mist; an image so breathtaking that it stopped all five friends in their tracks. They were totally unaware that their own silhouettes were also part of a very surreal picture, something noticed only by Matt, who stepped back to take a photo of this magical scene on his imaginary camera.

Now, almost twenty-five years later, the anticipation of what lay ahead was almost unbearable. It was seeing not only his friends but also the orphanage, the town and everything else that had made up the first eighteen years of his life.

Opening his eyes bought reality back to the present. It was already early Monday afternoon, and a very tired John still had a lot to do. He had to find some accommodation, get some sleep, eat and get cleaned up from his journey. He needed to be prepared for what could be the most important day in his life. John's car was soon back on the road, his journey's end now so close.

Chapter 8

Twenty-five years had brought a lot of changes to the outskirts of Mason. The Three Pines motor lodge was not an establishment John remembered. In fact, it was in a whole new area of redevelopment on the north-east corner of town. The motel looked quite new, warm and very inviting, but most importantly, it had a sign that said "Vacancy."

"Just fill this out, thanks." The elderly owner passed over a form and monogrammed pen. "Will that be Visa, Diner's or Amex?"

"Oh. . . cash. I'd rather pay cash. Is that okay?"

"Makes no difference to me, son, but I'll need your car registration as security then. Make sure you note it on the form."

John nodded approvingly, relieved that he didn't have to give any credit card details.

"You're lucky you came when you did. It's the last room I have," continued the old man as he motioned towards the window with a twist of his head and a raised eyebrow. "I only just turned on the vacant sign because I had a last-minute cancellation. Anybody coming later will struggle to find accommodation. There's a lot of folks in town for the display. Have you seen it before?"

John hesitated. "Um. . . a long time ago, I guess."

"You don't sound too sure, son! Guess you must have been quite young, eh?"

"Um, yes, I guess I was."

The old man took the completed form from John and gave it a quick look. "Just you staying, then?"

John's mind returned to the night before and his thoughts of Christine coming home with him, and now, how the old man had just said that it was his last room.

"Might also be my wife."

"Might also be your wife, then." The old man's repetition of John's statement made him realise just how unconvincing it may have sounded. However, the old man didn't seem bothered. He had obviously heard similar stories before, perhaps from the odd one or two travelling salesmen passing through, hoping a local bar might provide a one-night stand.

John knew, despite the logical half of his brain telling him he needed to rest – after all, it was probably going to be a late night – that he was just too excited to lie down and rest. So after a shave and a very hot shower to revive himself, he left the motel room for his car, armed with a new plan. He would drive around Mason to see what was new and what remained from the memories that he had as a boy. He couldn't wait to see Jennings' Hardware Store: would it still be operating? And the Main Street itself – there were sure to have been quite a few changes in twenty-five years, but what shops would still be there that he remembered? And, of course, the orphanage. If nothing else, it must surely still be there. John knew he had to do a drive past: it would be something that he could tell the others about later, in case they had only just turned up and hadn't had the chance to look around. John also knew that despite the fact that many food stalls would be selling mouth-watering treats later, he would need to stop for a nourishing dinner, so he planned to return the car to the motel after his drive around and then walk back into town, allowing time for eating before that all-important date.

Indeed, much had changed in twenty-five years. As he drove, John observed the differences in his hometown, starting with the hardware store. Jennings' had been bought by Arthur Cooper's, a hardware franchise that had over a hundred shops in three states. Being in the business, John was familiar with them and their tacky advertisements hosted by none other than Arthur Cooper himself, a larger-than-life individual whom John compared to a grossly overweight Colonel Sanders. Rumour had it that Arthur Cooper shared his life with an endless succession of attractive young blondes. *It's amazing what money can buy*, John thought to himself, cringing at the idea of any woman selling herself out to a man like that. And there was also their bright yellow signage, let alone the cheap inferior-quality Mexican and Taiwanese products they stocked.

Of all the companies to take over Jennings', why did it have to be Arthur Cooper's?

Most of the old buildings remained, but many with new owners. However, it was the redevelopment on the way to the orphanage that surprised John the most, with numerous commercial buildings now bordering the grounds of the still magnificent structure. From what John could see, the grounds appeared to still be well kept, but the gates at the bottom of the drive were firmly closed and locked. A large sign stating "Keep Out, Private Property" was not what John expected to see. In fact, he was a bit shocked, but found a small comfort in realising that at least it didn't say "Trespassers Will Be Prosecuted." The offending sign left no clue as to what purpose the building now fulfilled. Yet John was convinced that whatever purpose it now served, it was certainly not an orphanage anymore.

John stared at the building for a good ten minutes as distant memories of long summer days gone-by filled his thoughts. Perhaps the others would know what the new purpose of the Carlsson Orphanage was, or he might just have to ask around in town later.

It was just after six thirty p.m. when John started his walk to town from the motel. It was going to be a cold night, but he was prepared and suitably attired. As he walked, John realised that it was not just the cold but also the apprehension of what lay ahead that was making him shake. A good nourishing meal was certainly first on the agenda. During his drive through town earlier, John had failed to notice the eatery that he had planned for his evening meal. Perhaps his memory had failed him as to its exact location on Main Street, and he had missed it during his drive. His intention was to find it now, during his walk through town. Joe's Place, or JP's as it was affectionately known, was an institution in Mason, or at least it was in the sixties. Now, twenty-five years later, John struggled to find it.

JP's was the place where the cool kids hung out after school; the place where ice-cream sodas and their famous giant hot dog that could be ordered with up to ten different toppings were consumed by the kids with money. That was the kids who had real parents, certainly not residents of the Carlsson Orphanage. They couldn't afford the delicious-smelling treats that JP's served. John had only been there three times in his life: on his sixteenth birthday, his seventeenth birthday and once more, just before he left Mason. And now here he was, with enough money in his pocket to buy anything or everything on the menu. But JP's no longer graced Mason's main street; such are the ironies of life. Times certainly had changed, with the main street now hosting a collection of high-profile, fast-food outlets, each with its own glaring neon sign that mesmerisingly seduced and called out for you to turn your hard-earned dollars into corporate profits. But there was no way that the colonel, the clown, the funky-looking chicken or the man in the apron were going to tempt him. All their mass-produced offerings never came close to resembling the beautiful pictures placed seductively in the windows, and what you were served tasted the same whether you bought it in Mason, Pine Ridge, South America or Europe.

The fancy meal that he had planned for himself at JP's became just a hamburger and fries from the Lucky Lantern. Proprietor Eric Wong seemed pleased to take John's order. After all, John was the only customer at the time. The third-generation Chinese-American businessman certainly had stiff competition from the new corporate giants, but Eric made a good old-fashioned American hamburger, one that tasted just like a hamburger should. And as a bonus, he didn't try to upsize your order or sell your children any cheap plastic toys that would last little more than a day.

All the sights and smells – it had been so long, too long. Now with a full belly, John walked around, soaking up the memories, and although much had changed, there was still a lot that remained how he remembered it from twenty-five years ago. Mrs White's confectionary shop was now White's Family Bakery. Its beautiful lead-lighted window had long since been replaced with a single plate-glass sheet. John stopped and remembered how Mrs White would have a sticky donut for him in return for cleaning the shop window, whether it needed cleaning or not.

John knew that, with his new looks, he might be hard for his friends to recognise. Yes, there was the prearranged meeting later on, and then their get-together under the steps. But as John walked, he kept a sharp lookout, just in case his friends were doing the same thing. His eyes scanned the collection of people walking around in preparation for the festivities. Trying not to make obvious eye contact with anybody, he processed all the visible images that his eyes were relaying to his brain in the hopes of a positive identification, particularly of any blonde woman who looked to be in her early forties. Suddenly, his heart skipped a beat. There she was, on the other side of a stall. She looked so different, not like he imagined she would look, but those eyes, those big blue eyes. . . There was no mistaking who they belonged to.

John started to shake as he strategically positioned himself behind the woman, his trembling voice finally saying the opening line that he had practised so many times on the drive back.

"Did you ever find out who broke your little red pram?" Eleven words that would have meant nothing to anybody except Christine. She knew there was only one person who would say that and instantaneously turned around to greet her long-lost friend.

"Matt! How are you?"

It sounded so strange, given that it had been over twenty-three years since anyone had called him by his real name. Christine's outstretched arms were ready to hug his body as Matt embraced her in return, squeezing her tight. It was a hug that lasted a good thirty seconds, and Matt felt her warmth flow right through his body.

There was so much to say, but words didn't matter at that moment. The hug was just perfect on its own and could have lasted all night. Any thoughts of his life in Pine Ridge or the stern warnings about making contact with his previous life were a million miles away. Here she was, and so close, he could almost taste her perfume.

"I didn't know if you'd be here tonight."

"Christine, I would not have missed you or this for anything. You have no idea just how happy I am to see you. And you look so beautiful. You always were, but now, even more. . ."

As they'd talked, Matt had turned his full concentration to all things Christine, and there was nothing else in the world that currently mattered. A little voice inside was excitedly telling him that maybe the others wouldn't turn up and she would be all his. But Christine was on full alert for any of their missing friends, and she intermittently scanned the crowds as they conversed. It was only a few minutes before Christine suddenly pointed down the road.

"Look, Matt, it's Julian!" There was no mistaking the walk. His body was still slightly pitched to one side, but he looked really good and had put on quite a bit of weight over the years. Christine ran forward, closely followed by Matt.

"Julian, it's me, Christine!" Her arms reached out to embrace him with a force that nearly knocked Julian off balance. "How are you, Julian? You're looking really good."

"Good, thanks." Julian's brief reply wasn't unexpected, even after twenty-five years of not seeing his friends. He was still a person of few words.

"It's a good thing that Christine saw you, Julian." Matt put out his hand. "Great to see that you could make it."

Julian looked back blankly. Matt could see what he was thinking by the expression on his face... *Is that Matt or Adam?*

"It's me – Matt. Sorry about the change in my looks. It's a long story, but you look kind of different yourself these days."

Julian extended his hand. "Sorry, Matt. It's good to see you." Julian looked a little relieved it was Matt, and his apparent lack of excitement still did not seem out of place, despite the missing twenty-five years to catch up on, or thirteen hundred weeks, or nine thousand one hundred or more days. It was a long time, no matter how you looked at it. Julian showed little emotion and kept his words to a minimum; however, he did listen intently as the conversation drifted between Christine and Matt, who by now had come to accept he would not have Christine's full and undivided attention.

Matt could have happily spoken and listened to her until the early hours of the following morning. He didn't really care about the fireworks display, and now that Julian was there, it didn't really matter if the others turned up or not. He had waited so long to see Christine again, and now she was there. He was happy just soaking up her very presence. Then suddenly, the same little voice in his head told him that if the other two didn't make it, maybe they could ditch Julian. He felt bad about the thought, but it did increase his heart rate as he once again started to become aroused. Christine, despite being extremely excited to see both her friends, was still aware that there were two more people who needed to be found to complete the destiny of this reunion, and she continued to break eye contact to scan for any signs of Adam or Jenny.

Finally, she made the suggestion. "Let's walk down the main street, the three of us." Christine realised that Julian's distinctive limp might attract the attention of either Adam or Jenny, should they be walking around prior to the planned meeting on the steps.

Indeed, it wasn't long before a tall figure stepped forward from the slowly growing crowd. "Christine!"

Matt's heart sank as he watched Christine embrace a very different-looking Adam from the one engraved in his memory. As the seconds ticked by, Matt felt discomfort at the situation growing as he watched them embrace. Adam's hug appeared longer than the one he'd received from Christine. Did this mean that she missed Adam more than she had missed him? Matt was just on the point of getting ready to interrupt their embrace when, finally, Adam and Christine separated. He started to relax a bit. Adam now turned his attention to Matt.

"Matt, I'm so glad to see you, and I have so much to tell you. I've missed you so much, buddy." Matt and Adam embraced in a man hug, both patting each other on the shoulder in a show of masculinity. Matt arched his feet a little to increase his height. Adam was one inch taller than him, and elevating his height was something that Matt had done unconsciously whenever the two of them were around Christine. Now, even after all these years, he still did it without thinking. Suddenly, guilt took hold, bringing Matt back to reality. Having Adam there was now more than just okay. How could he possibly have not wanted Adam to be there? His de facto brother, best friend, confidant, comrade-in-arms; Adam was all of that, plus so much more.

The fact that Adam was now there would also restore the natural balance of things. Both men had always wanted Christine since adolescent hormones had kicked in, but like yin and yang, whilst they were both there, peace and equilibrium would reign. They would be brothers again, and Christine would be their de facto sister. There would be no awkwardness, either, with both unsure if a move on Christine would bring a receptive response or shock and horror.

Matt knew that despite his sad but erotically hopeful thoughts on the way down, this was definitely the best outcome. After all, even if Christine had been receptive to the advances that he would now never make, he would have had to lie about being married to Nancy. He didn't have to do that now, and he didn't have to live with the corresponding guilt. Reality had created a sense of relief.

There was so much to talk about, but the conversations that followed only seemed to cover the last twenty-four hours of what was, in reality, a lifetime. As the four friends made their way in the direction of the courthouse steps, the topic of conversation inevitably turned to if, or when, Jenny would be arriving.

"We should sit on the steps as they're elevated and would be the best place for Jenny to look for us. After all, it's our agreed-upon meeting place."

Matt, Adam and Julian were not going to disagree with Christine or her logic. The few extra feet gave the elevated advantage of scanning the countless faces that passed by. However, no one had noticed the slim figure that approached from the back. Both Matt and Adam jumped as a hand came down heavily on each of their shoulders.

"Bonjour."

A scarf hid the features of the person's face, but there was no mistaking the husky voice. It was Jenny, but not the Jenny any of them would initially recognise, as her now-removed scarf revealed shoulder-length auburn hair, not the short, boyish style they remembered her having. A small amount of makeup only accentuated her beautiful face, which was complemented by her expensive handmade clothes that would not have looked out of place on European royalty. She looked, quite simply, stunning. Both Matt and Adam stared quietly, speechless. How on earth could they have never noticed just how beautiful she was all those years ago? Was it just that Jenny had done such a good job keeping her femininity hidden, or were they both just blinded by their obsession with Christine?

"Jenny!" exclaimed Christine, breaking the awkward silence that had evolved. Christine leapt to her feet to give her friend a hug in the only way that seemed appropriate after nearly a twenty-five year break. Three more big hugs followed as the long-lost friends started talking to, and over, each other. Even Julian had started to participate.

"I am so glad to see you all!" Jenny smiled. "I was really wondering if anybody would turn up, especially after nobody wrote to me after I left."

"I wrote to you, Jenny! I sent you a letter just after you went away and one just before I left for my job. And Adam did, too. I remember Mr Carlsson said he would put both letters in one envelope and post it for us."

"I wrote to you, as well, several times, in fact. And so did Julian. And Mr Carlsson did the same for us, so you should have gotten them," Christine added.

"Well I didn't get any letters, but I did, of course, send you all lots."

"I never got any letters from you Jenny – none at all."

"Neither did I."

"Nor me. I didn't get anything either."

"Well, I sent you all letters and lots of pictures from France, so I don't know what happened. But this is not the place to talk about it. We must do this downstairs, under the courthouse steps, where we made the pact all those years ago. I put five bottles of wine down there this afternoon, ready for us, and I've been praying you would all turn up to drink them. This time, though, it's not the leftovers of half-drunk bottles – it's quality wine. That's one thing about living in France, you just don't drink cheap wine. So, everybody, follow me."

Indeed, it did seem the right thing to do as the four long-lost friends followed Jenny along the same passage where they had followed her all those years ago. Jenny flicked on the light switch as they entered the now musty room.

"Come in. I'll get the wine, and we will have a toast to old times. Then we have so much to talk about." Jenny looked puzzled as she reached for the wine bottles that were no longer where she knew she had put them. "The wine – it's not here. It's gone. Someone has–"

Her sentence was cut short as a figure stepped forward from the shadows, causing a minor commotion by knocking over a few old, abandoned items in the process.

"My dear, dear children, I am so glad that you have all come home." The voice and the figure were old, but they were still unmistakable.

"Mr Carlsson! What are you doing here?" Christine moved forward with outstretched arms, ready to embrace the old man. She was stopped in her tracks when Herbert Carlsson's right hand came out of his jacket clutching a gun.

"Stop right there! Oh, my dear Christine, you are as sweet as I remember, and so beautiful. I really don't want to hurt you, so please do as I say, or I will be forced to use this."

"A big joke. . . Jenny, I bet you put Mr Carlsson up to this, didn't you? Ha, ha, ha!" Adam gave a very unconvincing laugh.

"Miguel, please show my friend here that this is no joke." Adam sensed movement from behind him and started to turn, but it was too late. A large hand brought the handle of a gun firmly across the side of Adam's head, sending him crashing to the ground. Christine screamed, causing her captor to point the gun directly at her head.

"Now, we must be quiet, Christine. You see, I need you all alive. But if anybody tries anything stupid, then you, Christine, will be the first person I will shoot, and right between the eyes if I need to. So it's up to you and the others. I hope your friends have your best interests at heart."

Herbert Carlsson's comment was clearly aimed at Adam and Matt, as he knew a threat on Christine's life was the best way to get their cooperation. He moved forward until the barrel was only a few inches from her face.

"You will all hold out your hands because Miguel will be putting handcuffs on you. You see, we have a short trip to make, and I don't want any misbehaving from naughty boys and girls." The closeness of the gun to Christine's head was a very persuasive tool for cooperation, and it wasn't long before Miguel was leading the group outside towards the dark-coloured van parked in the alleyway. It was the same van they had passed on their way to the meeting place but that had given them no reason to think twice about it. Miguel did not really need a gun to be intimidating. Standing at six foot six and weighing around three hundred pounds, he was a big man with superhuman-sized hands. His scar-riddled face showed no emotion as, one by one, he forced the five friends inside, the last being Christine, closely followed by Herbert Carlsson, who was still holding the gun to her head. The interior light was the only source of illumination, apart from the small grille that separated the back of the van from the driver's compartment.

Once the door had been firmly closed, Miguel proceeded to the driver's side door, as Herbert Carlsson called out, "Okay, Miguel. We will go now."

Chapter 9

Miguel reversed the van slowly out of its parking space and down the alleyway before turning onto the main road for what would be the start of their twenty-minute journey. As they drove, Herbert Carlsson resisted all attempts to engage in any conversation regarding what was going on, except for a plea from a now tearful Christine.

"All in good time, Christine. We have something that we must do first, after which I will answer your questions. After all, I do owe it to you, but for now, you must all be quiet and try not to do anything stupid as I really don't want to hurt you, Christine."

Matt struggled to look through the small grille that divided the van's interior from the driver's compartment to get a glimpse of the outside world through the front windscreen; however, he soon realised that it was all quite pointless. Their position revealed only an occasional passing structure but no details of the road. Jenny sat quietly with her eyes closed; unbeknown to the others, she was drawing a picture in her mind of the van's course and position based on the turns that it made. Her thoughts were founded on getting her friends safely back to Mason, and figuring out where they were going would be a good start. But despite her best efforts, she had soon lost the mental map of where they were; firstly, because her mental map of the town was twenty-five years old, and secondly, because deliberately or not, the van had made many turns. The last forty seconds of the journey was unmistakably down a gravel driveway, and the opening of the van's side door revealed a rural setting, where they were parked next to a large barn. It was a cool, crisp evening, and the winter chill, compounded by fear, caused Christine to shake. Miguel soon had the large wooden doors to the barn unbolted, and as they opened, the pungent smell of animals drifted out like an invisible fog. The flick of a light switch revealed no animals, just an empty barn about eighteen feet wide and thirty feet deep, with twelve solid round posts rising from the floor to support the roof. These posts also functioned as dividers for the individual stalls.

"Inside, now." Miguel's abrupt manner caused Adam to hesitate as his anger had reached a point where he was finding it hard to keep it under control.

He quietly mumbled, "Asshole," but not quietly enough to be missed by Miguel.

With surprising agility for a man of his size, Miguel executed a swift kick to Adam's lower back, sending him crashing to the ground. His cuffed hands were unable to fully break his fall, causing his face to hit the ground hard.

"You're the asshole, and I said to get inside." Miguel's grin exposed an array of missing teeth. Herbert Carlsson watched as his accomplice secured each of the five friends, one by one, to the wooden posts. Only then did Carlsson feel secure enough to point the gun away from Christine.

"We will rest here for a few minutes while the good doctor does some quick tests to see if you are all indeed who you say you are." He turned to look towards the open door as a slightly built, elderly man stepped in. "May I introduce Dr Hintermann."

The man appeared to be in his late sixties or early seventies and spoke in a heavy German accent. "I will need to take some blood samples. I hope nobody fears needles."

"I hope you will all cooperate with the doctor," said Carlsson. "Remember that I still have the gun, and the first bullet goes through Christine's right kneecap."

With the blood samples collected, the doctor left the barn, followed closely by Carlsson and Miguel.

"We will be back shortly," said Herbert as Miguel closed and latched the barn door.

A brief moment of silence was followed by Matt and Jenny fruitlessly struggling to break free whilst Christine and Julian sat motionless, demonstrating acceptance of the situation.

Adam was the first to speak. "Okay, who blabbed? We should have been the only ones who knew about the arrangement, but they knew we'd be there!" His eyes looked towards the door. "Someone spilled the beans, so who was it?"

"It wasn't me," replied Christine quietly.

Adam turned his attention to Jenny, staring directly at her. He spoke pointedly. "Actually, I didn't think it was you, Christine."

Jenny realised what Adam was implying.

"No, no, no, it wasn't me! In all these years, I've told nobody!" pleaded a now visibly upset Jenny.

"Who arrived first and supposedly left some wine down there?" replied Adam.

"Honest, it wasn't me! For all I know, it could have been you, and now you're just trying to blame me so no one suspects you!"

"Stop!" screamed Christine. "We're supposed to be friends; look what's happening to us."

Matt, always the logical person, stepped into the conversation to back Christine up. "Christine's right. I don't think anybody blabbed. We have to find out how they knew and why this is happening. What this *does* explain is why all of our letters went missing. If he read them all, maybe he discovered our plans for the reunion. But I'll tell you that I made absolutely no mention of it in my letters."

"Well, I didn't say anything about it in my letters, either."

"Nor me; absolutely nothing."

"And I most definitely didn't. It was part of our agreement not to write it down or talk about it."

Jenny turned to Julian. "Julian, was there anything in your letters that could have led Mr Carlsson to find out about our reunion?"

Julian looked very worried as he realised everybody was looking at him. He shook his head as he replied, "No, absolutely nothing. I'm not that stupid."

Matt continued from where he'd left off. "I believe we're all telling the truth. The important thing is not how Carlsson knew we'd be here, but *why* he's so interested in holding us captive. I think we should each tell what's happened to us since we last met, then we might be able to work out what's happening. And I'm happy to go first."

Matt's idea hit an agreeable chord with everybody. Even Julian showed excitement at hearing the other's stories. It wasn't long before Matt had condensed the last twenty-five years of his life into five minutes, including his time at the army base, his relocation to Pine Ridge, his new identity, the hardware shop and the trip back to Mason. Quick and factual, that was Matt. There was complete silence as his friends absorbed his story like sponges. His tale had captivated his audience.

"Well, that's my last twenty-five years," Matt wrapped up. "Now, what about you, Adam? What's your story?"

Adam took a deep breath before relating his experiences over those years. He told his friends how after his time at the base with Matt, he, too, was given a new identity; that of Phil Clinton, an identity he grew to hate over the years. Phil was married to a woman named Daisy; the marriage produced no children, however. He met Daisy two years after his relocation to a small town in Missouri, and together, they ran the garage that Phil had the opportunity to buy with funds mysteriously bequeathed to him. After working there together for several years, where Daisy ran the accounts and administration whilst Phil and another mechanic, Bart, ran the workshop, they eventually split, which left Phil devastated. Phil knew it was his fault. He'd been restless since he'd left the army base. Something that happened there had left him empty and searching for answers, which led to him shutting his wife further and further out of his life. When he realised how bad he'd become, it was all too late; she had left and started a new life. At first, the situation left Phil so depressed that he fired Bart, sold the garage and started to spend a lot of money on alcohol. Eventually, he pulled his life back together, and then Phil found he had a natural ability with women. He started on the first of many new relationships, with sexual conquests becoming simply a numbers game. Although he lived in a modest apartment, he found himself living a life that most red-blooded men could only fantasise about.

However, despite all the excitement that his lifestyle gave him, there was something inside that just never felt right, and it was something he just couldn't work out. Phil still fulfilled his obligations to the organisation. He did, however, miss a doctor's appointment – once. But after walking into his apartment the following day and finding a picture of Daisy that had been cut in half, with a handwritten note detailing a new appointment time and the words "Don't be late," Phil made sure he never deviated from what was agreed to again.

Daisy was now remarried, but Phil still cared for her deeply. Like Matt, he knew he had to make the reunion, but was aware that there would be repercussions if he was found out: he now feared that by making the trip, he might have put his ex-wife's life in danger. As Phil, Adam had put together a plan that would explain his absence. He had, over the last year, started to make regular trips to quite innocent locations. He'd hoped that would dispel any suspicion about him being away now. The plan, however, didn't allow for a lot of time to make the return trip, and Adam had planned to leave no later than midday the following day in order to return in time. Now he feared for not only his own life and the lives of his friends but that of his ex-wife, as well.

Matt had an uneasy feeling. If Adam had put Daisy at risk by attending the reunion, he had probably done the same to Nancy.

"Now, Christine, tell us your story."

"No. Sorry, Adam, I want to go last. Julian and Jenny can go before me. So, tell us, Julian what has happened to you since we last met?"

Julian's story was, to be expected, short and softly spoken. "After my time with Christine at the base in North Dakota, I was given a new identity."

"What happened to you at the base?" Adam interrupted abruptly.

Adam's comment was met with a blank stare from Julian, and Christine quickly stepped into the conversation.

"It's okay. I'll tell you about what happened at the base when it's my turn." After catching Adam's attention, her face indicated not to push the subject.

"As I said, I was given a new identity and a new occupation in Phoenix, working in a bookstore that I was later given the opportunity to own." Julian went on to tell how, with the new name of Martin Robertson, he'd been married once, a long time ago, and only for fifteen months. "It was not a good marriage," he continued. "We had no children, but that's okay; neither of us really wanted any, anyway. I was quite relieved when it ended."

"I'm sorry your marriage didn't last," exclaimed Jenny with genuine empathy before she took her turn. "And now I guess I should tell my story. Things were great in Paris. I missed you guys so much, but Jean Michel's parents made me feel like the long-lost daughter that they never had. Jean Michel was the love of my life, and we never wanted to be apart. His parents would take us to their holiday house, and we would go shooting in the forest. Jean Michel's father was a keen hunter, something that Jean Michel did not inherit, but I thoroughly enjoyed it. So he participated for my sake. We were married in the family's church and lived in the upper apartment of his parents' house. When his parents died, we took over the whole house. It was too big for us, although by then, we had our daughter, Louise. She was so beautiful, with long blonde hair and big blue eyes. She reminded me so much of you, Christine. In fact, when I saw her just after she was born, I wanted to name her Christine, but we'd already picked the name Louise. She would have been almost twenty-one today."

"What do you mean 'would have been?'" Christine's question sounded rather anxious.

Jenny paused a few moments before replying. "She was thirteen years, two months, and four days old. It was a wet evening. Jean Michel had collected Louise from ballet, and on the way home, there was an accident. Their car was hit by another; it caught fire, and they were trapped inside. Another driver managed to smash the window and get Louise out, but Jean Michel died right there in the car. Louise died two days later from her injuries."

"Oh my God! Jenny, I am so sorry." Christine desperately wanted to comfort her friend, but she was well and truly attached to the post.

"It's okay, Christine. It was a lifetime ago now. I was devastated beyond belief, but I had thirteen beautiful years with her and seventeen beautiful years with Jean Michel, and I treasure every one. No one can take that or my memories away from me. I still struggle with what happened, but time slowly heals, and one day, I will see them again. I truly believe that, and knowing that comforts me. Now, Christine, I think you should tell us your story."

Jenny's story was far from finished, but considering what she'd just told them, nobody felt it appropriate to push her for further information, although they all were wondering about what happened to her more recently, specifically the seven years between that horrific event and their meeting in Mason.

Taking over from Jenny, Christine coughed to clear the lump that had formed in her throat. "After Matt and Adam left, things were just not the same. I was concerned about looking after Julian and leaving Mason, but Mr Carlsson approached me one day saying a colleague had a job to offer, just like the one Matt and Adam had got, but he assured me that this job was more suited to me and Julian. We spent only a short while at the facility in North Dakota, when on that day, that dreadful day, we were separated and given new identities. I didn't know what to do. I was so worried about Julian. I felt it was my duty to look after him, but they assured me that if we cooperated, we'd both be well looked after. If not, then Julian and I would both be regarded as anti-American and treated accordingly. I had no choice, so I was reborn as Carla Reed, a young woman starting her working life in Oregon. I guess I was well looked after. A good job, an apartment and a bank account. I had everything except happiness, and I had lost my four best friends. I often cried myself to sleep thinking of wonderful summer days growing up in Mason. I tried to find comfort in the arms of my male work colleagues – young, old, married – anybody who would listen or showed me some affection but they, of course, only ever wanted one thing, and when they got what they wanted, they weren't interested in me anymore. I was married once: I thought it was love, but I was so wrong. I became just one of his possessions, like his cars. After we split, I went from relationship to relationship; most were just one-night stands. It's a miracle I never got pregnant. I don't know what I was looking for, but I had to keep searching. There was something missing in my life, and I was foolishly trying to find it through human interaction. One cold, rainy evening, I was out walking, thinking about taking my own life and how I could do it. I concluded that jumping from a bridge was the easiest option because once you let go, things were out of your control. At the time, it seemed like the only way I could find what I was looking for. I just kept walking and walking, and soon, the neighbourhood became unfamiliar. I was soaked to the skin and very cold, but I kept walking. It was then that I met the man who changed my life."

By then, Matt had become very agitated. Despite the seriousness of their current situation, he'd become filled with jealousy thinking about all those other men who'd had the pleasure of being intimate with Christine, men who probably only ever saw her as a sex object and didn't love her, not the way that he could have loved her if life had turned out differently. He realised he wanted her so badly, but deep down, he knew he'd never have her, and now he had to hear about the love of her life. It was all too much, and without thinking, he abruptly interrupted.

"Who was he? Did you marry him?"

Christine smiled. "No, Matt. It's not like that at all. That night as I was walking, I saw a partly open door, and there was a light and strange warmth I just can't explain coming from inside. It drew me closer. I walked up to the door, knocked and then pushed it fully open. Sitting there with his back turned to me was a pastor. Unbeknown to me, I'd walked into the back door of a church. He turned around, totally unsurprised to see me. His first words were 'Please close the door and have a seat; I've been expecting you.' We talked for several hours. He knew things about me that nobody else could have known, things that still amaze me. He changed the way I looked at everything, and that day was the first day of the new me." Christine looked down at the cross hanging from a chain around her neck. "This is the most important thing to me these days. Now I don't have to waste my life searching for what I'll never find or be tormented by what's going on inside me. I spent all those years thinking I had no parents, when all the time, I had a father in heaven who loved me unconditionally. I just had to give my life to him. Now, I have a father I can talk to anytime. That night, the pastor gave me three verses. They meant nothing to me at the time, but he told me that one day, they would make sense. I know that time will be soon."

"What were the three verses?" enquired a puzzled Jenny.

"Not yet, Jenny, but soon. It won't be long before I'll be able to share them with you, and I will, but only when the time is right."

Jenny was just about to question Christine further when the latch on the barn door clicked and the door burst open. In walked Miguel, now holding a gun. He made several tormenting gestures at Adam, gesturing as if to shoot him. Miguel was immediately followed by Herbert Carlsson and the doctor, who both stood in the doorway.

"Oh, my children, my dear, dear children. What interesting lives you have had since leaving the orphanage. I had Miguel install a microphone in anticipation of you telling your stories. I have waited such a long time to hear them, but now, the good doctor has informed me that you are indeed who you say you are. So now we must go, as we have a long drive ahead, and time is getting on."

Herbert Carlsson had barely gotten the words out when out of the shadows of the door appeared the arm of someone holding a gun that was pointed directly at his head.

"Get your fat friend to drop his gun on the floor, or this bullet is going to go right through your head!" exclaimed the female voice.

Carlsson replied, "Miguel, do as the lady asks. Quickly now, please."

Miguel hesitated before finally dropping his gun to the floor.

"There we go, my dear. Just as you requested. And now, may I ask who you are?"

Chapter 10

The slim figure stepped forward into view, and Matt recognised her immediately.

"Nancy, what the hell are you doing here? How did you know? Did Lana tell you?" The expression on Matt's face was a mixture of surprise, shock and outright horror.

Nancy turned to Matt; however, she did not appear very pleased to see him. "You have the cheek to ask me what I'm doing here? What the fuck are you doing here? And who the fuck is Lana?"

In all the years that he'd known Nancy, Matt had never heard her swear. "I. . . I had to meet–"

Nancy didn't allow Matt to finish his sentence. "Just shut it, John. I don't want to hear any excuses. I bet you have no idea what you've gotten us into. We had everything; we would've been good for the rest of our lives. All you had to do was stick to what the agency asked of you, but no, you had to come and meet some old friends! You have no idea how you've totally fucked up big time. You've put our future and our lives literally at risk! For what? To meet some old friends."

"How... How do you know about the agency and the agreement? You couldn't have known."

"Well, John, isn't it a night of surprises? So here's another one for your dumb brain to think about. I used to work for the agency. Why do you think Marty was so keen for you to hire me? I was assigned to look after you and make sure you didn't do anything you weren't supposed to do, but stupid me, I fell in love with you. Now, that was definitely not supposed to happen. I really tried not to, but God help me, I did! I knew that I couldn't watch the man I was married to, so I gave it all up, my whole promising career, for you, for love, and this is how you repay me!"

"But how did you know I was here?"

"I didn't, John. But when you talked about meeting old buddies, alarm bells went off. I made you promise not to, but I was still concerned and knew I had to act in case you did anything stupid. I still have some old contacts, so with a bit of help from an old friend, I placed a long-range tracking device in your car and a shorter-range one in your shoe, although I did lose you a couple of times on the way. Between the two of them and a lot of luck, here I am. Surprise!"

"And Mr Carlsson and Miguel? Do they work for the agency as well?"

Nancy gave a half-hearted laugh. "What, Laurel and Hardy here? You've got to be joking! I don't know where or how they fit in, but I wouldn't take them seriously. Believe me, at the moment, they're the least of your worries." Nancy's words were an invitation for Herbert Carlsson to speak.

"Nancy, it's so nice to meet you. My name is Herbert Carlsson. You, of course, know your husband as John, but for the first eighteen years of his life, I knew him as Matt. You see, Matt and his friends are all orphans, and I ran the orphanage where they grew up. In fact, I would like to introduce you to his friends."

"I'm really not interested, so why don't you just shut up."

"But, my dear, I think you will be very interested. You see, Adam, Jenny and Julian are his friends, but Christine here is the true love of Matt's life." Herbert waved his hands to introduce an embarrassed-looking Christine.

"That's enough. Now, let's get the handcuffs off of John." Nancy did not seem pleased by Carlsson's declaration.

"No, really, my dear. Since he was a boy, Matt has been infatuated with Christine. I have watched him and Adam grow up competing for her affections, neither able to bear the thought of the other having her. And they probably never even realised how obvious they were."

"That's enough, old man. We've been happily married, and we only want to be with each other."

Matt wanted to correct Nancy's collective "we" but thought better of it.

Ignoring Nancy's rebuttal, Carlsson continued, "Now, I bet he married you to help forget about her. In fact, I would guess that every time he made love to you, it was Christine he was thinking about. So let's ask Matt if it is true and see if he can deny what I just said."

Nancy's gun remained firmly trained against Herbert Carlsson's head, but she turned her body towards her husband. She didn't have to say anything as her expression said it all. Nancy was waiting for Matt to deny what Herbert had said. She watched Matt's mouth open, but no words came out.

Matt felt his face go red and hot as he realised everyone was looking at him and waiting for a reaction. His mind went through the available scenarios. He could deny what had been said, but that would be the biggest lie he'd ever told. Or worse, it could be just what would bring Christine and Adam together. He could tell the truth and hurt Nancy, who was already angry and was the only person in possession of a gun. But at any rate, he really did love her and didn't want to hurt or lose her. The remaining option of changing the subject wasn't practical, as eight sets of eyes were watching him; even Miguel and the doctor seemed to be interested in his reply. It was only seconds, but it felt like minutes, and still no words came out of Matt's open and suddenly very dry mouth.

Nancy broke the deafening silence. "Well, tell us, John, or should I say. . . Matt."

Still, Matt's words remained frozen as his heart beat faster. With everybody focused on his reaction, nobody noticed that Julian had freed himself from his handcuffs and grabbed an adjacent piece of wood. Suddenly, he made his move, lurching forward. Nancy's peripheral vision picked up his movement, and she instantaneously swung the gun around just as the wood came down, hitting her right forearm and sending her crashing to the ground. The gun departed her hand and slid across the floor towards Miguel, who quickly bent down to pick it up and pointed it at Nancy.

"I am not Laurel, and I'm not Hardy. I am Miguel; don't forget it." The stupid expression on Miguel's face following his statement was more appropriate for a cheap comedy show, but it was Herbert Carlsson who again took the floor.

"Thank you, Miguel. And thank you, Julian! Now, let's see. My, my, how the tables have turned. What a pity that we never got to hear Matt's reply, but I think that we all know the answer." Herbert smiled, while Jenny looked at Julian.

"Julian, what's going on?" Jenny queried.

Julian said nothing but, instead, turned to look at Herbert Carlsson, who once again took control of the conversation.

"Jenny, Jenny, Jenny... Have you not realised that this Julian is not *your* Julian? In fact, his name isn't even Julian. But so many names, Matt, John, Karla, Christine, and it's just so confusing, I think we should just call him Julian."

The realisation hit Jenny that if this person was not Julian, then what had happened to him? Was he dead? Or perhaps he was being held captive somewhere.

She lashed out. "You bastard! Where is Julian? Is he okay?"

"So many questions, Jenny, but we don't have the time for answers at this moment. You see, we have a long drive to make, so I will make you a deal. If you cooperate, then nobody will get hurt, and I will answer your questions on the way."

Adam called out in an angry voice, "We're not going anywhere with you, and there won't be any cooperation with anything unless you start giving us some answers!"

Herbert looked at Adam with a pathetic smirk before replying, "Adam, you are not in a position to negotiate. You seem to be unaware of who is tied up and who has the guns, so let me make things clear for you. There is an easy way to do this and a difficult way; perhaps Miguel can demonstrate the difficult way."

He signalled to Miguel, who needed no further encouragement. He delivered a high blow to Adam's stomach, causing him to lurch forward, saliva spewing from his mouth. Miguel was just about to deliver a second punch when he was stopped by Carlsson.

"That's enough, Miguel. I think he has the message now, and after all, he is worth nothing if he is dead."

Miguel seemed disappointed but refrained from delivering the second blow.

"So, then, is there anybody else who is not going to cooperate?" Stunned silence followed Carlsson's question. "I thought as much, so this is what's going to happen. Miguel will take you, one by one, and restrain you in the van, starting with young Nancy here and finishing with Christine, because if there is any sign of non-cooperation... well, I have already told you about Christine's lovely kneecaps."

It took about ten minutes for Miguel to load Nancy, Jenny, Matt, Adam and finally Christine into the van. Each had their handcuffs attached to a cargo restraint that had been previously fixed to the middle of the van, which left them very little room to move. The doctor and Herbert Carlsson also sat in the back, with Herbert positioned directly at a right angle to Christine. He knew too well that a gun trained on her was the best way to ensure calm and cooperation from the others. Julian got into the front passenger seat next to Miguel, who put the van into gear and started the long drive that lay ahead.

The van's interior once again offered no clues to its final destination, which now seemed somehow irrelevant. The only thing that felt important was reversing the situation and escaping. Matt's, Adam's and Nancy's minds were working overtime going through their limited options.

"Okay, Carlsson, we've cooperated, so tell us." Jenny's words were sharp and to the point. It was the first time in her life that she had omitted the title 'Mr.'

"Where is Julian? And what are you doing with us?"

"Calm down, Jenny. We have plenty of time to talk, and I am a man of my word. I will answer your questions. I think it is only fair that you should know. So, let's start at the beginning. Five years ago, I was approached by Dr Hintermann. The good doctor had himself been approached and offered a considerable sum of money to find anybody who had been part of the project and was still alive."

"The project!? What project?" Jenny interjected.

"Dear, Jenny, please, no interruptions. It is very rude, and I will not tell you anything else if you interrupt again."

"Okay, sorry," she replied sheepishly.

"Now, unfortunately, I could not help the doctor as I did not know where you had all gone. And for two years, I thought nothing of it. Then, three years ago, I met up with young Paul Collins. You may remember him – he was about four or five years younger than you."

Jenny and Christine both quietly nodded.

"Well, young Paul certainly remembered Julian, or more specifically, Julian's limp. So when he spotted a slim man with a funny walk working in a bookshop just outside Phoenix, he was convinced that it was Julian.

However, his approach was met with a blank stare and denial of the name, but a very intuitive Paul knew that it really was Julian, although he didn't push the point at the time. Luckily for us, he passed the details on when we met. I immediately contacted the doctor, who confirmed that the monetary offer was still on the table, and we negotiated the deal and how we would split the money should I locate you."

Jenny's mouth opened, but she thought better of speaking and closed her mouth before any words came out. She didn't want Herbert to stop divulging the details.

"I know how close you are, and I was convinced that if I could find Julian, he would be able to lead us to the rest of you. So with the help of my good friend Miguel, we found Julian in the bookshop, just as described by Paul. And we... well, how should I say this without upsetting you, Jenny? We took him for a drive to a deserted location for a little chat. Miguel is a man of many talents, one of which is the ability to extract information from people. Surprisingly, even with Miguel's special skills and tools, Julian was an extremely hard man to break. It took two hours with Miguel leaving Julian barely inches from death before he finally broke, and once broken, it all came out: your pact and your reunion. Such a loyal friend – most men would have given up in a fraction of the time he spent with Miguel. Who would have thought that of Julian? I take my hat off to that young man. I will never think of him as weak again! So, Jenny, you of course want to know what happened to him."

Jenny nodded, her eyes open wide and full of tears.

"I am afraid that what Miguel had to do to extract the information was too much for the poor boy. He passed away about an hour later. We really did try to keep him alive as he was worth money to us, but alas, the injuries were too much for his body to cope with."

Jenny's eyes filled with more tears and her throat went dry. Anger and thoughts of revenge filled her mind, but she knew it was not the time or the place. She would have her time, and revenge would be sweet.

Herbert Carlsson's tone suddenly changed from sad to excited as he continued with his explanation. "As I said, as sad as it was to lose Julian, all was not lost, for I knew how to find the rest of you. I just had to wait three years – three long years! However, it did give me lots of time for planning. One problem for us was how we would recognise you. But then I had an idea so brilliant, I astounded myself. If we had our own Julian, then you would find *him*! That's where Andre played the part so brilliantly of the frail limping man. Such a good actor who will soon be well paid for his academic performance. Losing Julian was not actually so bad for us, as just like you, Christine, he was worth only a fraction of what Adam and Matt are going to bring us. You two are going to make the remainder of our lives very comfortable. Jenny, I am sorry you are worth nothing to us financially, but unfortunately, just like Miss Nancy, you have to come along for the ride."

"So where are you taking us, then?" Nancy questioned.

"All I can say is that we have a long drive to meet some acquaintances."

"Then tell us this, why are we worth money?" Matt asked. "Does it have to do with the project you talked about, which I presume was our time with the army? What the hell did they do to make us so valuable? You have to tell us."

"My dear Matt, if I could answer that question, I would. I honestly do not know why you are worth so much money, but I do suspect that there are two people who can answer that question. One is, of course, the good doctor, but he won't tell you. I know; I have already asked him. The other is, of course, young Miss Nancy. Perhaps you can tell us what we want to know!"

Matt looked to Nancy. "Tell us, then, what have you been hiding from me all our married life?" For the first time since seeing her at the barn, Matt felt in control of the situation. Six pairs of eyes in the back of the van turned to look at Nancy.

Chapter 11

Nancy cleared her throat and composed herself for a few moments. She felt on the defensive, which seemed ironic given it had been she who had attempted to come to the rescue. She was now fired up, and unleashed at Matt.

"Anything that I ever failed to tell you was to protect you, but you know what? I don't know anything about your past prior to meeting you, except that John Dobson was not likely to be the name you were born with. For whatever reasons, the agency had interest in you. I know they had your best interests at heart. They wanted you safe to live a good life, a life that you have now destroyed, not only for yourself but for me as well. So, there you go – nothing. I knew absolutely nothing about your past, and until today, I didn't care. But now, I do care, because what remains of our lives depends on us getting out of this mess. It's not me but the doctor who holds the key, so perhaps, Doctor, you can tell us what this is all about?"

The doctor slowly shook his head before quietly replying, "No, I don't think that is a good idea."

Silence filled the van. Everybody was looking down except for Nancy; she stared at the doctor for a few moments before speaking. This time, her voice was calm, and her words were well thought out.

"I know exactly what you mean, Doctor. As you know, I also worked for the agency. I know all about not divulging restricted information and the consequences of breaking procedures. We've both been indoctrinated into the ways of the agency; something that these others wouldn't understand." She indicated the others in the van with a toss of her head.

"We both know, however, that you have already crossed the line. It doesn't really matter now if you tell us everything, because by dealing with these people, you are as guilty as if you had already told all your friends. In the agency's eyes, you've already told us, so you have nothing to lose. I think some of us may not be here twenty-four hours from now. I believe you are an honourable man, Doctor, and as such, you will grant us an explanation as a last request."

Nancy's calm voice and wise words made an impression on the doctor. He thought it over before slowly and quietly starting to speak.

"Before the war, 1937 to be exact, the German government found itself in possession of certain material. Given enough time, this material could have changed the future of mankind. Some forward-thinking men at the time realised the possibilities, and I was funded to start work on a project that would captivate me to this day. However, at the time, the science in this field was in its infancy, and we made very little, if any, progress. Without the results that our backers demanded, our funding dried up. However, as the war dragged on, interest in the research picked up again. The few people who knew what we were doing also realised the unparalleled power of where we were poised. If only we could have mastered it. Had we been successful in our research, the outcome of the war could have been very different, and the potential results could have complemented the Führer's vision of a perfect Aryan race. Time was not on our side, however, and with the arrival of the Americans, I was eventually taken to a military base with what remained of my team, here in America, where we carried on with our research under the guidance of our new masters. We worked in a very limited capacity until 1947, when America also found itself in possession of similar material."

The doctor paused to catch his thoughts, but his captivated audience egged him on as to what this special material was.

"Genetic material," he replied boldly.

The expression on Matt's face said what they were all thinking.

"Yes, young man – genetic material, very similar to you and me, but with one difference. . ." The doctor briefly paused again before continuing, "By technical definition, I would struggle to classify the material as human."

Adam balked. "Doctor, am I supposed to believe a story like what I think you're trying to tell us? I'm not that gullible!"

"Adam, let the doctor finish; this is very important." Christine's words settled Adam. "Please, Doctor, carry on," Christine urged.

"What I said is true. The specimens were so similar that we started our initial research by carrying out experiments on death-row prisoners and street people – the sort of people no one would miss or cared about. Nobody survived more than a few days, but we learnt a lot, and with the discovery of a new generation of anti-rejection drugs, we embarked on a new phase of our research. Now subjects could have small amounts of replacement tissue introduced over a period of time and survive. You see, in the early trials, it was all too much for a human body to accept. The two lots of antibodies would attack each other, but with access to the new suppression drugs, I had some of my biggest breakthroughs as we developed a process that allowed the body's defences to accept the introduced material without compromising the immune system. This initial program was called Project Neptune. With regular small exposure to the genetic material, the recipients would adapt and become both better and stronger. However, things were far from perfect because the subjects had to be kept in a controlled environment."

"So, are you trying to tell us that we were part of that project?"

"No, not that project. That phase of the research was done only on army personnel, but it did not have what was deemed to be an acceptable success rate. Our research was continually adapted to eventually become Project Neptune Five and Neptune Six. This was where the project took a whole new direction.

"Up to then, the whole project was the army's dirty little secret, as they imagined legions of super soldiers. However, all in the world is not what it seems. The army works for the government, but the government does not work for the people. Instead, it is controlled by an elite group of people who have the real power. When there are billions of dollars at stake, even the most watertight vessel starts to leak like a sieve. You see, the world had changed, some were asking who needed superhuman soldiers when wars are now fought with guided missiles and nuclear bombs. The research could offer power and wealth beyond measure for those who controlled it. The agency was given oversight of the research, and they thought the project was at a point where it could be taken totally outside of the military. There were unimaginable amounts of money to be made and a lot of political pressure from the few people who were privy to the project. But the military did not want to lose their baby and still saw military implantation as the main goal; after all, old enemies are always being replaced with new ones. There was huge political pressure applied from both sides, and what happened was a bit of a compromise as the project got divided. Two projects, two agendas – one controlled by the military and one by the agency, but running side by side. The military wanted quick results, but the agency's plan was always a long-term project with candidates they could monitor and observe. They did not want people confined to the control of the army. In fact, they wanted a variety of normal people of all different shapes, sizes, gender and age. People who could fit into everyday, normal society. They wanted to see how you would adapt over the years, but they had to have the right people. They wanted people with no family, who could be given a new and controlled life. Why? Because they believed if a person had no past, then they could create a false past and mould them a new future, one that the agency could monitor and participate in. Matt and Adam, you had just completed Phase One and were almost through Phase Two. Christine and Julian were only part way through Phase One, so Christine, although you are of great value, it's really all about Matt and Adam. You can't begin to imagine how much monetary value you two are to us."

"Why are we worth money to you? This doesn't make sense," Adam replied indignantly.

That prompted Herbert Carlsson to reply. "Adam, believe me, you and Matt are worth more than gold to us. Christine, alas, is only silver, but still of value. Perhaps the doctor can explain. I am also interested in finding out why."

"Once your antibodies combined and your bodies adapted, you became stronger people, not in physical strength but rather in your ability to fight off infections unlike a normal human being. Imagine, no colds, no flu, instant bounce-back from major infections or injury, a superhuman immune system that could confer an extended life expectancy, or even your body being able to fight off and kill cancer cells before they can spread. That is where the real money is. Do you have any idea what people would pay to live twenty years longer or to cure their cancer? Or more to the point, what an organisation will pay to be able to offer that to people?

"The only irony of the project was that while we had produced superhuman beings, anybody taking part lost the ability to reproduce, something we just couldn't make sense of, and it's still something that we are working on solving. Think about all those medical check-ups you had. Every time you had a visit to the clinic, they would take tissue and blood samples. Your blood was worth more than the finest champagne, but it was all controlled by the agency, or rather, what is left of the agency.

"You see, in 1966, something went horribly wrong. As the army wanted quicker results, their candidates were taken down different paths of development. Some of these paths went too far too quickly. There were mutations and deaths, but one case spun dangerously out of control. What happened as a result had the potential to destroy human life on earth as we know it.

The situation had to be contained quickly, and contained quickly it was! The whole project was shut down overnight; both the army's and the agency's parts were terminated. I believe that all the soldiers who were taking part in the army's side of the project were killed off in a series of accidents. What happened was too much, even for the puppet masters. Even they realised that there was no point in controlling the world if there was no one left alive to control.

"Now, here is the interesting part. All of the participants in the agency's project, including the four of you, were also killed off. So how are you still here, alive?" The doctor raised his hands in a mock symbolic gesture of disbelief.

"Well, it was actually four people similar to you who were killed. You see, we knew there were no problems until at least Phase Five of the project. You four were not dangerous or a threat, and you were too valuable to kill off, so your deaths were faked. Now the department was officially going to close that part of the agency down. After all, why would it be needed if all the subjects, yourselves included, were dead? So within the agency, an elite group was set up to monitor you and the other eight people who were deemed too valuable to be destroyed. Yes, a secret group within a secret group, with links that went right up to the top. However, with the whole project officially disbanded, they could not keep you as such, and in a bold move, they reverted to the original plan and gave the twelve people who had survived new lives and new identities before dispersing you around the country. Only this time, for a slightly different reason.

"The financing and power behind all of this was a consortium of drug companies who didn't know or want to know what they were investing in, but rather what they were going to get for their money. I believe that many people in the agency who were involved in the monitoring – and I guess this includes you, Nancy – had no idea they were working for a group within the agency that officially didn't exist. After all, you don't ask questions, you just do what you are ordered to do. I guess you just assume that what you are doing is for your country, don't you?"

The doctor turned to look at Nancy, who slowly nodded her response.

"Now, a rival group has offered us an incredibly large amount of money for the three of you. You see, they somehow found out that you still exist – something the department itself still doesn't know. To hide a secret this big, only certain people can know certain things. I knew, of course, of your existence because I received your regular samples, but I did not who you were or where you lived. I also knew that, out of the original twelve people, only nine were still alive. That, of course, became eight after Julian's unfortunate demise. When I was approached, I could only dream of the money that I was offered, and I didn't believe that I could possibly supply what they wanted in return.

However, I did my research, and in the process, I found Mr Carlsson. He turned out to be a dead end because he also did not know where you were. So we both thought all was lost. But then there was Julian's discovery. All we had to do was wait, and our financial dreams would come true."

Herbert Carlsson had a big smile on his wrinkled face. It was obvious he wanted to interrupt. "Thank you, Doctor. Most of the story I never knew myself. All I really knew was that if we delivered the three of you, we were going to be really rich, way beyond my wildest imagination, and to be honest, that is all I care about."

Adam huffed. "Well, I still think this whole story is a lot of crap. It's flawed. Right from the start, you said that what you had could change the outcome of the war, but now you say it's taken forty-five years to make people healthier. You've totally contradicted yourself, Doctor. And as for everything else – well, really!" The look on Adam's face clearly told the doctor what he thought.

"I have no reason to lie to you. What we believed at the time could have changed the outcome of the war. However, nature presented us some unexpected challenges. If we knew then what we know now, things would have been very different. I was only involved on the medical side, but the same source of the samples also provided us with access to technology that we were only just starting to master by the end of the war. I had contacts and heard many stories about the other items that we had come to possess but were still learning to control when the Americans arrived. Your government took everything back to America in what must have been the biggest cover-up of the whole war. After that, we heard nothing more of the amazing technical wonders that Germany once had in its possession. Given enough time, those are the things that could have changed the outcome of the war. Another two years, young man, and you would have grown up speaking German! *Mama, ich bin ein stuppit Amerikanischer junge.*"

Adam was indignant. "Sorry, Doctor, but you're full of crap. Have you any evidence? Of course you haven't. I've heard nothing from you that comes close to being believable. As for your country, Nazi Germany was evil and thankfully lost the war."

"Young man, you are so naive. Do you really think your country is any better? I knew my country was doing many evil things that I could not condone, but I was a proud German and did what I had to do for my country. Now I am an American myself. Your country knew what I did, but they still offered me citizenship, a new identity and research facilities. In return, they wanted my knowledge, skills and control of my research. You have no idea what your government gets up to. You would be very shocked and surprised!"

"At least my government is not a bunch of Nazi bastards! And I still think you are full of crap, just a silly old man living forty-five years in the past."

"Stop!" Christine, who had been quiet to that point, suddenly got everybody's attention. "I believe the doctor is telling the truth. You see, it all makes sense now."

To the others' surprise, Nancy piped up. "Okay then, Christine – if the doctor is telling the truth, does that mean you are Nephilim?"

"No, Nancy. We were born of human parents, so we can't be."

"I'm sorry, but who or what the hell are 'Nephilim'?" Adam looked puzzled.

"They are talked about in the Bible, in Genesis," Christine replied. "The Nephilim were genetic hybrids around the time of Noah. They were the offspring of human and supernatural beings and were superhuman, but despite their strength and size, they could not reproduce."

Christine now turned her attention back to the doctor. "The genetic material that you talked about, where did it come from?"

"I really do not know, and it was never my place to ask. I was supplied with it, and I played God with it. I only believe in that which I can see and touch. You three are living proof that I created genetic hybrids myself, so that concept is not fantasy, but I do not believe in Nephilim or any of the other children's stories that your Bible talks about. In fact, I choose not to believe in God at all because I know I have played God with what I have created, and if I was to believe what your Bible says about monsters like me, then nothing short of hell and eternal torment awaits me.

"I choose, instead, to believe that death holds nothing more than a black void for everybody. So while you are alive, you should enjoy life to the best that you can, and with the money that I will soon have, life will be more enjoyable than I could ever have imagined."

Christine replied, "It is never too late to repent, Doctor; everybody can receive forgiveness. I can show you how."

"Thank you for your concern, young lady, but believe me, it is far too late for me. You have no idea what evil I have done."

Jenny asked, "Christine, you said it all makes sense to you now. What did you mean? Please tell us."

Christine looked back at Jenny. Now was the time to start sharing. "I meant that the first two of the three readings now make sense." Christine paused before reciting the prophetic words that had puzzled her for all these years.

"The first reading was, '*God looked down upon man and he was pleased with what he saw.*' And the second reading was, '*No bird in the sky or beast in the field shall bear fruit with the son of Adam.*' Can't you all see? We were all created perfect in God's eyes! We now have something foreign inside us, something that should not have been there. That's why only you, Jenny, have been able to bear children. What is inside us will die with us."

The silence was overpowering before Jenny finally spoke again. "I believe the doctor, as well. This is all way over my head, but what I do know is that you do not mess with God or nature, so you must tell us what the third reading was, please, Christine."

"Sorry, Jenny. Now is not the time, but soon. The time will come soon."

Adam felt a cold shiver flow through his body as the constant drone of the van carried them closer to their fate.

Chapter 12

Matt found it hard to estimate how late it was. He could not see his watch clearly in the semi-darkness of the van's closed interior. Normally, he had a good sense of the passing of time, but the events of the evening had totally clouded his judgement. Matt surmised that it must have been at least four hours since they had left the barn to when the van made a sudden sharp right-hand turn before driving down a steep and uneven track for about five minutes before coming to a stop. The opening of the side door by Miguel now filled the van's interior with the sound and smell of fresh running water. Wherever they were, it was certainly a very secluded area; the dirt track had led to a flat grass bank adjacent to a fast-running stream. As the cold chill of the night air now also filled the van, it only added to the fear of the unknown that all the captives held inside.

"Now listen, everybody. We have a short stop to make as we need to gas up, and this is an opportunity to go to the toilet if needed." Herbert Carlsson's words broke the air of anticipation. "And may I add that if you all cooperate, I have some hot coffee available." Carlsson indicated to Miguel to release Christine, but freedom was short-lived as Miguel re-secured her to the front bumper. Herbert Carlsson's gun remained continually trained on her head. Now that Christine was secure, he informed the others of his plan. "Miguel will help remove you from your restraints in the van, one at a time, starting with Matt. The handcuffs will remain on, however, and remember that I have Christine right in my gun's sight."

Miguel assisted Matt out of the van and undid his zipper so he could relieve himself. Once Matt was re-secured in the van, it was Adam's turn. With a sick sense of humour, Miguel produced a small stick and caught Adam midstream, causing him to urinate on the front of his shirt before coming to a stop. Instinctively, in a fit of anger, Adam kicked out at Miguel, sending up a small cloud of dust harmlessly in his direction. Miguel just stepped back and, surprisingly, did not retaliate. The fun of seeing Adam humiliated was rewarding enough and required no further action.

Carlsson said, "Ladies, I know this is awkward, but I am sure we will all look the other way."

"You have to be joking!" Nancy didn't try to hide her utter disgust at Herbert Carlsson's statement.

"I'm okay," replied Christine calmly.

The same could not be said for Jenny, who was bursting. "I need to go! Please undo my cuffs so I can have some dignity. I promise not to do anything stupid, and I will do what you say."

Herbert motioned for Miguel to remove Jenny's cuffs. As promised, she fully cooperated, knowing that Christine's safety depended on it, and she allowed herself to be re-secured in the van.

Miguel turned his attention to recovering the three large petrol containers that had been hidden beneath some undergrowth. He spent around ten minutes refuelling the thirsty van's tank. Two large thermoses of coffee were produced from the front compartment. Miguel passed around a plastic cup for the captors to drink from. The coffee was warming and well received; however, continuing his torment of Adam, Miguel managed to get only around a quarter of the coffee into Adam's mouth, while the rest went down his shirt and onto the crotch of his trousers.

"You bastard!" Adam spat what he had in his mouth at Miguel, who once again just laughed. The humour of the situation was again enough for his satisfaction.

"Ooops. So clumsy of me," replied Miguel as he gave Adam one of his partially toothed smiles.

Christine had spent fifteen to twenty minutes outside, secured to the front bumper. The winter air brought a chill that penetrated right through to her bones. As the van door once again slammed closed on the captives, she found herself shivering uncontrollably, something that had not gone unnoticed by the others. How Matt longed to hug her and keep her warm. He looked over at Nancy, and she looked back, seemingly knowing what he was thinking.

A few minutes into the drive, Nancy broke the silence. "I hate to be the bearer of bad news, but we all are screwed, no matter the outcome. If they haven't already, the agency will soon realise that at least one of you is missing. And when they see all three of you are unaccounted for, how long do you think it will take them to put two and two together and look for the common equation – your hometown? As I see it, if they get to us first, the old boy here and his three stooges will be history. The three of you will be kept secure until they figure out what to do with you. And remembering that you're not supposed to exist, your chances of any form of freedom are not good. Now, as for me and Jenny, they can't let us go because we know far too much. The best outcome would be that we are detained for the rest of our natural lives, but I think, in reality, we'll just disappear. There's no way they can let this get out publicly. The other scenario is that we're given to the bad guys, you three would again be kept in a laboratory, and Jenny and I will probably just be disposed of since we appear to be of no value and are just liabilities."

Nancy turned directly to Matt and took a deep breath before continuing. "I might as well tell you now, since I might not get another chance. I would rather that circumstances were different and that there was no one else listening, but I guess it doesn't matter now. What

I'm about to say is something that I really need to tell you. Perhaps it's something that I should have told you many years ago. When I was sixteen, I had a baby girl. Quite a potential scandal in those days for an unmarried girl in a small town. My parents told everybody that I was staying with relatives on the East Coast, but in reality, they had made me a guest at the Sisters of Eternal Mercy. Can you believe that? The Sisters of Eternal Mercy! We weren't even bloody Catholics! However, for the right-sized donation, the sisters were happy to take care of my parents' small problem. The reality was that it was the most horrible time of my life. It was like a prison. Even though I was pregnant, I was expected to work hard, some sort of penance for our sins, and those who didn't follow the rules were appropriately punished by the nuns.

"When Lilly was born, I didn't get to say goodbye to my daughter. They wouldn't even let me touch her. Parents had already been found for her six months before she was born, and she was taken straight from me as soon as the cord was cut. I knew right from the start that it was the wrong thing to do. It took a long time before I could even bear talking to my parents again. I guess they knew it was the wrong thing, as well, but by the time they realised, it was too late. After Kenney's death, I was their only hope to become grandparents. After we were married, I thought it would be good to have them close, perhaps a new start for us all. I had said a lot of bad things to them before I left home, and I needed to make amends. I wanted them close so that they could be around for our children when they were born. I never thought it would be a problem; after all, I had gotten pregnant so easily the first time. All the years that I couldn't conceive with you, I knew that it couldn't be me, but I couldn't tell you how I knew without telling you the whole story."

"Oh, I thought you. . ." Matt struggled to finish his sentence.

"You thought it was me, didn't you? Well, sorry to burst your male-ego bubble, but now you know. However, I guess it doesn't really matter any more, does it? In fact, it is perhaps a blessing. No children who will be worrying about their parents' disappearance."

An awkward silence filled the van as Matt reeled from Nancy's second blow.

Chapter 13

Nancy's words about their possible fate had sunk deep into Adam's mind. He knew he had nothing to lose as he pulled hard and violently against the bar that his handcuffs were secured to, causing then to gouge into the skin of his hands. With excruciating pain, he lunged violently forward, and the pain travelled up through his arms as the skin on his wrists started to tear.

"You bastards! You'll pay for this."

Herbert Carlsson's reaction was nonetheless quite calm. "Adam, if you don't behave, the doctor has something in his box of tricks that will make both you and Matt quite controllable. We will give it to you if needed, and remember Christine's value is not going to decrease if she becomes a cripple."

"Calm down, Adam." Jenny's words were stern and to the point, causing Adam to sit quietly.

"Thank you, Jenny. I am glad he listened to you as I really don't want to hurt anybody. After all, we are almost family."

"Family, my arse." Adam gave a symbolic spitting gesture.

A moment's silence was broken by a calm Christine. "Mr Carlsson, there is something I just don't understand. We were family; you were a substitute father, the man who loved and cared for us. You were a good man, and I believe that inside, you still are a good man, so why are you doing this? If nothing else, please tell us."

"You really want to know?" Herbert Carlsson replied. He paused before continuing as Christine nodded.

"I think you may have already made up your minds about me, just like everybody in Mason did. The only difference is that you must now think I have turned into a horrible monster. Well, perhaps I have!"

"Please, Mr Carlsson, I know you're not a horrible monster. Tell me what happened," Christine pleaded.

"Okay, Christine, if you really want to know. We were family. I was the grandfather you never had – your big brother, your guardian. I gave you everything at the expense of living my own life. I never married nor had my own children. Every cent that I had went into the orphanage, and when state laws changed in the seventies, it made running the orphanage a legal and financial nightmare. I slowly but surely cashed in my investments to keep things running. Some of my remaining assets were lost in the Mason County insurance collapse in the early eighties, leaving me in a very compromising financial situation. However, I kept the orphanage running, not for me, but for the children still living there.

"Then there was that terrible day. . . that is, Lorna Willis, who was trouble from day one. But when she made that horrible accusation, most of the town made up their minds. I would never in a million years even contemplate what she claimed that I did. The thought still makes my stomach turn in disgust. That is how she repaid me for all that I did for her. Yes, I was eventually found not guilty, but by then, the damage was done. When I walked down the street, I could see what they were thinking. Why would a middle-aged man want to run an orphanage? The fact that most of the staff were women and it was Mrs Appleton who looked after the girls was irrelevant. I had lost everything, including the respect of the town. Ultimately, the mayor's wife led a campaign to close the orphanage."

"Mayor Castleton's wife?" inquired Christine.

Jenny was thinking to herself with total amazement, *Mrs Appleton is still alive? Surely not!*

"No, Christine, there have been a few mayors since Jim Castleton. It was one of his successors, Mayor Kenney Hackett, and his wife, Joan. Yes, the lovely Joan Hackett – man-hating, feminist, lesbian bitch that she was. Kenney was just a token mayor. She was the real power behind him, manipulating everybody and everything for her own benefit, including Kenney. However, what she accomplished was only to bring forward the inevitable. I lost everything, and I mean everything. So, what did I get in return? Perhaps a warm fuzzy feeling knowing that I helped so many boys and girls over the years to grow up, ready to face the world as stable mature adults? I lost count of the pupils who left and from who I never heard again. How many of you remember my birthday? Come on, tell me."

No one replied to his question.

"Well, I remember all of yours. If not your actual birthday, then the one you were given at the orphanage. Yes, every single one of my past residents. Miguel has been my only real friend. He came to the orphanage many years ago, needing a job, and later, even when I could not afford to pay him, he still stayed, like a loyal friend."

"Loyal dog," muttered Adam quietly.

"So, when the doctor tracked me down and told me about the offer he had been presented with, I was intrigued. A while later, after hearing about Julian's possible location, I had to really examine my life and what I wanted for the rest of the years I have left on this earth. You can think of me what you like: I actually don't care anymore. I have spent my whole life doing things for other people, and where did it get me? Nowhere. So I made my decision.

"It was time that I lived for myself and not for others. I am an old man. I probably haven't got many years left, but with the money that I will be getting shortly, rest assured that they will be good years. I can buy a brand-new Porsche, have a long holiday in the

Caribbean and I can sleep with as many pretty young ladies as my money can buy. For the first time in my life, I am going to be free to do something for myself, and if anybody gets hurt in the process, well – I am sorry, but that's the way it is!" Herbert Carlsson paused for a moment, allowing Adam to comment.

"You really are trying to justify your actions, aren't you? Well, keep trying to convince yourself. You might even believe it. We, however, can see you for what you are." The look of disgust on Adam's face said it all.

However, Christine looked sympathetically at Herbert Carlsson for a few moments. She said nothing, instead closing her eyes, and her lips moved gently as if she was quietly praying.

But Herbert Carlsson hadn't finished justifying his actions. "You see, Christine, when you have seen as much of life as I have – well, let's just say that life has shown me two things. Firstly, nice people are the ones who miss out, and haven't I learnt that lesson! Secondly, the only person who has your best interests at heart is yourself, you and you alone. Even if a person genuinely cares for you, they still primarily have their own interests at heart. We are each in control of our own destiny, and I don't want to be lying on my deathbed thinking how I spent my life benefiting others but missed out on what I really wanted in life, like cars, fun, good food, good wine and lots of pretty women by my side. I am not Mother Teresa, so now I have hopefully answered your question."

Total silence had filled the van as the four friends reflected on Herbert Carlsson's words and how time had changed him. This was not the same man that they had known as children.

The long straight road slowly changed, turning into several gentle climbs, with the road twisting to the left and the right. It was as if they were climbing several high hills or small mountains. Later, after several more turns onto more minor roads, the van suddenly came to a stop. Miguel once again got out and opened the side door.

"The doctor has to make a quick phone call, so no stupid moves." Herbert Carlsson stepped aside to allow the doctor out of the van, but his gun remained constantly trained on Christine.

The doctor's phone call took less than five minutes, and he was soon climbing back into the van, where a quick nod and smile was acknowledged and returned by Herbert Carlsson.

"Okay, Miguel, let's go."

Miguel obligingly put the van into gear.

"Not long now," Carlsson continued to the van's other occupants. "The final part of our journey."

Glimpses of the new year's morning light were masked by the growing darkness of increasing storm clouds. The rain had started not long after they left the area where the doctor had made the phone call, and it had steadily increased in intensity during the last part of their trip. Every drop was amplified by the lack of lining on the van's steel roof. Matt still had no idea of the exact time, but felt it had to be at least five thirty when the van made a sudden sharp left-hand turn onto a gravel road. Matt guessed that they were now on a private roadway, because Miguel had stopped to open a gate.

"Leave it open," called out Carlsson though the grille that divided the two compartments. He had to almost shout to be heard above the sound of the rain on the van's roof. Thunder could be heard in the distance as the van started its slow climb up what had become a steep gradient.

The van's flat sides were hit with a few gusts of wind that noticeably rocked the vehicle. Without warning, the van's interior momentarily lit up with light coming though the grille. Despite the limited size of the only window that faced forward, the light was intense, the result of a lightning bolt hitting a tree not far from the side of the driveway. The noise was deafening. Miguel instinctively swerved away, to the left, causing the van's forward left-hand wheel to move over the edge of the driveway. Feeling the wheel suddenly drop, Miguel, who was still partially blinded by the lightning, forced the steering wheel to the right, but it was too late. The van started to slip down the side of the hill, and applying the brakes only caused the wheels to slide on the soft surface. A sudden bump sent its occupants up from their seats. Miguel had no control as the van headed towards the stream at the bottom of the hill.

Suddenly, there was a loud bang, and the sound of breaking glass accompanied the van's deceleration as it swung violently to the right.

Matt vaguely remembered the sounds of women's screams when the van flipped onto its right-hand side and slid a short distance before dropping down an embankment, causing it to land upright with the front-end semi-submerged in the stream.

Following the screaming, everything else was just a blur for Matt until there was a slap in his face and the sound of Nancy shouting. "John, wake up! Are you okay?"

Matt mumbled incoherently. He remembered feeling a strange warmth over his face that he would later realise was blood from a head wound he'd sustained in the crash. But at the moment, he just wanted to drift back to that peaceful feeling, the same one you get just before entering sleep.

But Nancy was now shaking him. "John, wake up! You've been hit on the head. I'll be back in a moment. Hang in there, John."

Matt drifted off again. This time, it was the sound of both Nancy and Adam that roused him. He recognised Adam's voice but struggled to make sense of what he was saying.

Adam started shaking Matt. "Wake up, buddy. We have to get to the house."

"No. Let me go to sleep."

"Matt, are you okay?" Adam sounded extremely worried about Matt's drowsiness. "Hang in there, Matt. I just have to help the others, but I'll get back to you."

A container of cold river water did for Matt what Adam's shaking couldn't do.

"What the hell?!"

"Welcome back, but you deserved that after the shit you got us into."

"Nancy, what happened? God, my head hurts."

"You took a nasty hit to the head; we need to get you somewhere safe and get you cleaned up."

As Matt roused from the last few blurry minutes that the hit on his head had induced, the events of the evening slowly came back to mind, as if he were waking from a dream. The reunion, the abduction, Nancy turning up and now the crash. Of course, the crash.

"The others – how is everybody? How is... I mean, how are you?" Nancy was well aware that Matt's first thoughts were of Christine's condition, but she passed along no comments about her.

"Adam and Jenny are okay, but like me, bloody shaken. The doctor and Carlsson are alive. Jenny has Carlsson's gun and is watching them, but I don't think they will give us any more trouble."

"And Christine? How is Christine?" Matt could not contain his concern any longer.

But it was Adam who would answer his question after he entered the van.

"I'll just be outside," Nancy indicated to Adam, stepping outside as he entered.

"Adam, tell me how Christine is!"

"She's not good, Matt. When the van went over, the door broke away and cut her quite deeply down the side of her body. Jenny is with her. She and Nancy have wrapped the wound to try to stop the bleeding, but we've got to get her somewhere safe where we can get her wounds cleaned and dressed. And we need to treat your head wound, as well. You look a mess. There's a house at the top of the hill. It appears that's where we were heading. I've just spoken to Carlsson. Evidently, there's no one living there. We must get you guys to safety."

Matt struggled to make sense of what Adam was saying. He'd obviously not gotten his full concentration back following the crash. Matt suddenly realised that his hands were not restrained by the handcuffs anymore.

"Adam, my hands are free. How did the handcuffs come off?"

"I haven't got time to explain everything, as we must get Christine to the house. But during the crash, the securing bar broke away at the back. I wasn't able to slip my cuffs around the broken bit, but Carlsson had been thrown from the van and was shaken up. With my foot on his throat, he surrendered the keys. I was then able to free everybody. Now come with me – we must get to the house."

Matt's thoughts suddenly turn to Miguel. "Where is Miguel? Has he got the other gun?"

"Miguel is dead. It looks like a tree branch smashed through the windscreen and hit him right between the eyes. The front of his head was opened up. And Julian's impostor isn't much better off; he's still alive, but he's trapped. The whole front of the van has been pushed in, and his legs were squashed. He won't be going anywhere; in fact, he's barely alive. I don't think he'll last long. I have Miguel's gun. Now, listen to me, no more questions. We must get you and Christine up to the house."

Matt felt Adam's strong arms pull him out of the van. The air was cold and damp.

Nancy turned around to look at Matt. "I guess Adam has told you about Christine. We need to get you and her to the house."

Nancy turned to Herbert Carlsson, who was sitting on the ground with his hands over his face. She kicked him in the back, causing him to lurch forward.

"Get up old man; lead the way to the house."

Herbert Carlsson struggled to his feet. He was obviously still shaken and slightly dazed as he stumbled forward. Nancy turned and, pointing the gun at the doctor, said, "You, too, Doctor. Move your ass."

The doctor stumbled to his feet and followed Carlsson.

"Not so tough any more, are we?" Adam called out. "Not without monkey boy to watch your backs. But the bastard has got what he deserved."

Adam felt justice had been served with regard to Miguel's violent demise. He assisted Jenny with bringing Christine to her feet. Supporting her on both sides, they proceeded to help her move forward. Christine struggled to walk; she appeared weak and very unsteady. Matt wanted to be the one who was helping Christine, but he could barely walk himself. He turned to look at the front seat of the van. There wasn't much left of Miguel's face. Matt now found himself staring at Andre, the man who had played his friend Julian so well.

Andre's attention was focused on Matt as he struggled to produce faint words. "Please don't leave me to die. Please!"

"Matt, follow us. Don't worry about him; he'll be dead soon."

Matt turned to follow Adam. Despite all that had happened, Matt felt bad. It must have been the pathetic look on Andre's face, a look that would haunt Matt for the rest of his life.

He turned back one final time. "I am sorry, but I can't help you. I have to go."

It was a long climb to the house. Despite the slow pace of Adam and Jenny assisting Christine, Matt only just kept up. It was Herbert Carlsson, the doctor and

Nancy who reached the front door of the house first. They waited for the others to catch up.

Chapter 14

Adam pushed Herbert Carlsson forward with his free hand, while Nancy held the gun to the back of Herbert's neck. Adam instructed him to knock on the door, but Herbert Carlsson hesitated.

"I said knock."

"There is really no point, Adam," replied Carlsson. "I have already told you that there is no one at home, no one here at all. That's why we have come all the way out here."

"Are you sure? Or is this another of your lies?"

"No, Adam. There is no one here. The farm belongs to Miguel's cousin, who is currently in Mexico. The distance from Mason made this place a perfect location for our transaction to take place; we wanted somewhere that could not be connected to us. Even Miguel's cousin would not have known we were here if it had all gone according to plan."

"Stand back," exclaimed Adam, as a solid kick from his right foot sent the door crashing in.

"We have to get Christine inside," he said as he once again helped Jenny move Christine, this time into the living room and onto a big couch in the middle of the room.

Nancy proceeded to have another look at Christine's injury. "It looks like quite a deep puncture wound," she explained. "I am reluctant to undo the bandage; at least it's stopped the bleeding."

"Doctor, get over there and have a look." Adam pushed the doctor forward.

Doctor Hintermann slowly released the homemade bandage and blood started to ooze from the wound. "It appears to be reasonably clean, but we have to keep the pressure on it as it still wants to bleed, and she has lost quite a bit already." He proceeded to retighten the dressing.

"We must get her to the hospital!" exclaimed Jenny.

"Yes, she does need medical help. But unfortunately, it is not that easy. If we take her to a hospital, it's only a matter of time before the authorities will be able to find us."

"That doesn't matter; we must get her to a hospital," Matt cried out.

Nancy exploded. "It doesn't matter! John, you still have no comprehension of what danger we would be in, do you? Listen, the authorities will be after us, let alone the acquaintances of the old man here. Speaking of which. . ." Nancy turned and pointed the gun at Herbert Carlsson. "Who exactly is coming here?" she asked. Herbert Carlsson hesitated, and Nancy moved the gun closer to his forehead. "I asked you a question, and we haven't got time to wait for your answer."

Carlsson relented. "His name is Carter. That's all I know about him. The doctor's been dealing with him, not me."

"When is he due here? And how many people will be with him?"

"I don't know how many people are coming with him, but it will be soon. In fact, I am surprised that he is not here already. The agreement was that we would meet; they would collect Matt, Adam and Christine and give us the money. We would then go our separate ways. The doctor's phone call was to give Carter the exact address, as we had only told him the approximate area and where to wait for the phone call. We wanted to make sure that we got here first. We had planned it all so well."

Nancy's gun rotated to the doctor. "What do you know about this Carter man, then, Doctor?"

"You don't mess with him, lady. I have only met Carter once, and he scared me. He said if we turned up without you, we would be very sorry. I tell you, Carter and his associates make the mafia look like a nun's tea party. And as Herbert just said, they will be here shortly."

"Oh, fuck!" she exclaimed.

Matt noted that this was, in fact, the second time in his whole life that he had ever heard Nancy swear.

"Okay. Listen, everybody." Nancy stopped to collect her breath before continuing. "We have to get Christine to a doctor, not a hospital. But before we can do that, we have to deal with the men who are coming for us. From what we've just been told, it sounds like we haven't got a lot of time. As I see it, from what your friend Carlsson and the doctor here have said, the people who are coming are expecting to collect two men and one woman, and that is what we can show them when they arrive. If we, that is, Matt, Adam and Jenny, are waiting for them with Carlsson and the doctor, then I can be hiding from the side with one of the guns and hopefully we can take control of the situation. We would have the element of surprise; I think it's the only chance we have."

"Have you ever shot anyone?" enquired Jenny.

"No, I've not actually shot anyone, Jenny. But I have had substantial firearms training with the agency."

"Could you kill someone if you had to?" Nancy hesitated at Jenny's question, allowing Jenny to continue. "Well, I've never shot anybody, either. But I have shot lots of birds and animals in the forest. I never miss what I aim for. If I must shoot someone, I will. And if I have to kill someone to protect myself or a person I love – then I will! You act out the part of Christine and I will hide, because if I need to shoot, I will, and I can assure you I won't miss."

Nancy hesitated before agreeing. "Okay, Jenny, but I'll have the second gun and I'll be behind the doctor and Carlsson."

"I think I should have the second gun," interrupted Adam. "After all, I'm a man."

Nancy turned to look at Adam. "Have you ever even fired a gun?"

Adam's expression said it all.

"Look," said Jenny, pointing. The elevated view from the front of the house revealed the tell-tale beams of headlights from a vehicle turning into the driveway at the bottom of the hill.

"Quick," called Nancy. "Take your places. I pray that they don't see the van on the way up." She motioned towards the doctor and Carlsson. "You realise if we don't pull this off, you are both dead, so I trust you will cooperate."

They both nodded in acknowledgement. The big black Lincoln slowly pulled up the driveway. The car had been slightly stretched to accommodate an extra row of seats, and all the windows were tinted, obscuring any view of the inside. As it stopped, the back door opened, and a solidly built man slowly started to get out. He was holding a black leather briefcase. The man was soon joined by two others. All three were dressed in very expensive looking dark suits, and they were quite tough-looking characters.

"Ah, Doctor, I see you made it," said the man holding the briefcase. "It is good to see you again, and I see that you have three presents for me. I certainly hope for your sake that they are the presents I have been expecting. If they are not, the people I work for will be very upset, and that would make me upset." The man looked towards Herbert Carlsson. "You must be Carlsson."

Herbert Carlsson nodded and held out his right hand in anticipation of a handshake, a gesture not reciprocated by Carter, the man holding the briefcase.

"Where are your two other helpers, Doctor?" asked Carter, looking around for Miguel and Andre.

"They are resting inside," replied Carlsson nervously. Carter looked at Herbert, the expression on his face not changing. "I didn't ask you. I was asking my friend, the doctor." He turned to the doctor, who just remained silent.

"Something is not right here; I was expecting three presents and four of you, but I only see two of you. I am also not happy that my presents look a little bit battered. Why is he covered in blood?" Carter pointed at Matt. "So, Doctor, something is not right. You will tell me what it is." As Carter uttered the last words of the sentence, his right hand reached beneath his coat and brought out a gun, an action mirrored by his two accomplices.

The bullet from Jenny's gun found its mark, a human head being a bigger target than the small birds she had practised on numerous times during family hunting trips in the French countryside. The man to

Carter's left fell instantaneously, his finger that had been poised on the trigger releasing a bullet harmlessly into the air as he fell. Carter and the second man, swung around to the left, firing in the direction of the fatal shot.

Nancy made her move while Carter's attention was diverted to the left, and her bullet hit Carter in the right forearm. The gun dropped from his hand as he leaned forward in excruciating pain. Jenny had the sense to drop to the ground immediately after executing her fatal shot, so she was hidden amongst the undergrowth, and the shots that were fired in her direction travelled harmlessly inches above her. With a deep breath, she composed herself for her second shot, catching Carter's second accomplice in the chest as he tried to break cover behind the Lincoln. The accomplice fell to the ground, only seconds remaining of his allocated time on earth.

Adam rushed forward to retrieve the gun that was lying by his side, whilst Nancy did the same with Carter's gun.

Carter, who had fallen to his knees, proceeded to slowly stand up; even with a shattered arm, he looked a menacing subject. "You lot are in big trouble. My people will hunt you down like animals. You don't know who you are dealing with." Despite three guns aiming at him, Carter seemed unfazed by the situation. Instead, he just repeated his statements about them being in serious trouble.

"We have to get out of here." Nancy turned to Carter. "Where is the money? We know about the money."

Carter started to laugh and pointed to the briefcase lying on the ground beside him. "It's in there, of course, you stupid bitch."

Nancy picked up the briefcase and tried to open it. "What's the combination?" she yelled at Carter.

"One, four, seven," replied Carter, now laughing cynically. Nancy adjusted the three combination wheels on each side, releasing the two latches and allowing the lid to spring up. She looked at the content for a few seconds before throwing the case and its contents at Herbert Carlsson. "This is what they were going to pay you for betraying your friends."

Herbert Carlsson felt his heart sink as he looked at the case's contents of neatly bundled, blank pieces of paper cut to the size of monetary notes that had spilled out.

Despite his pain, Carter continued to laugh. "You stupid old man, do you really think that we would have let you walk off with that amount of money? The only thing I had for you was a bullet; in fact, three bullets – one for you and one each for your two missing colleagues."

"And the doctor?" Herbert Carlsson was aware that Carter had not yet mentioned him.

Carter turned to Doctor Hintermann. "You can tell him if you like, Doctor."

"Herbert, you really are a stupid man. You have no idea of the consequences of what we've just done. I was originally not going to tell anybody the reason why the three of them are worth so much money. But after Nancy said what she did, I got to thinking and realised that within a couple of hours, everybody who was in the van except four of us would be disposed of. Because my three patients would be detained very securely for the rest of their lives, it would actually be safe to tell you all."

"So, you knew what was going to happen."

"As I said, Herbert, you really are a stupid man. Of course, I knew. Just like you have betrayed your friends, you have been betrayed yourself. Do you really think that you or the others could just walk away from all this, knowing what you do about the events of the last ten hours? Even if I hadn't told you the reason for their value, the three patients and I are the only ones who would be leaving with Carter. I wouldn't be safe leaving here; the agency would soon track me down. So, in exchange for my help, Carter's employers are going to give me a new identity overseas, and it was going to be me – not you – who would be having as many pretty ladies as money can buy. You said in the car that only nice people miss out. Well, Herbert, you must have been very nice during your life."

The doctor laughed before continuing. "Everything I said in the van was true except for one thing: just one tiny little detail. You see, it wasn't them who approached me; it was me who approached them."

Carter turned first to Herbert Carlsson. "The doctor is the one I had the agreement with – not you, old man. And he is the only person who is of any use to us."

He then turned to Jenny. "All that you and your friends have done is extend your life by a short period of time. We now know who you are, and by the time my associates have finished with you. . . well, let's just say you will all wish that you were dead."

"Great!" shouted Nancy. "No money, an agency that is going to hunt us down to protect its secrets and these guys who also want us. I guess it's just going to be a case of who gets us first. We have no money to run with and nowhere to run to." Her head turned towards Matt; he knew exactly what she was thinking.

"Nancy is right," replied Jenny. "But we do have one thing in our favour; these three are the only ones who know what we look like." She tossed her head towards Carter, Herbert Carlsson and the doctor. Nobody picked out the true meaning of Jenny's statement and what she was alluding to, and before anybody could comprehend Jenny's meaning, two quick shots rang out from the gun that she was holding. The first one caused Carter to fall backwards, blood running out of his chest. As she swung around, the second bullet caught the doctor. This one found its target a bit higher, penetrating his neck and causing his head to flick to the right-hand side. The doctor fell lifelessly to the ground. Jenny now had her gun trained on Herbert Carlsson, who was shaking violently and had uncontrollably wet himself.

"That leaves just you, Mr Carlsson." Jenny was staring him directly in the face.

Matt moved forward. "No, Jenny, not Mr Carlsson. You can't."

Jenny never heard Matt's words; she was fixated on Herbert Carlsson's face as she looked at the man who had once loved her as a daughter. She stepped forward, now only around eighteen inches from his head.

"This is for what you did to Julian, you bastard."

The bullet entered the front of his head, causing the rear to explode in a shower of brain matter and red pulpy tissue. Jenny stood motionless. She didn't watch his body fall because her eyes were still focused on the point where his eyes had been seconds earlier. Jenny's hands let go of the gun. She had just experienced an adrenaline rush like no other, and the reality of what she'd done and its consequences now began to register in her mind. For right or wrong reasons, she had just killed five people, and with this knowledge, she, too, started shaking uncontrollably. She felt dizzy and started falling forward. She would have landed hard had she not been caught by Adam and Nancy, who both grabbed her tightly.

"What have I done?" she wept.

Meanwhile, Matt stood motionless in disbelief, and his eventual words sounded quite pathetic. "But that was Mr Carlsson. . . You've killed Mr Carlsson. Jenny, you've killed Mr Carlsson."

"Shut up, Matt. She did what she had to do." Adam's words were stern as he helped steady a still visibly shaken Jenny.

"Jenny did the right thing," echoed Nancy. "Adam is right; she did what she had to do. They were the only people who knew who we really are and what we look like. We now have a chance, a very slim chance. We must get out of here and get as far away as we can. We need a good head start, and we still have to get Christine to a doctor."

In all the excitement and tension of the present events, Matt and Adam had momentarily forgotten about Christine, still lying injured on the couch inside.

Chapter 15

Matt and Adam rushed into the house, Adam kicking the door open as he rushed through.

"Oh my God!" Adam was first to enter the room, but he was halted in his tracks by what he saw. The sofa where Christine lay, including the sheets that had been placed over her, were completely red. Christine had moved whilst she had been alone, and her wound had reopened. Matt and Adam were soon followed by Nancy, who was supporting a traumatised Jenny. Nancy had done basic medical training as part of her requirements at the agency, and she immediately rushed to check the open wound. Nancy knew from experience that a little blood goes a long way, but she also knew that this was more than a little blood. Matt and Adam, still recovering from the initial shock of seeing Christine like this, had positioned themselves on either side of her. Each held one of her hands.

"Nancy, how is her wound? Can you help her?" pleaded Matt.

Applying pressure to Christine's side to stop any further blood loss, Nancy looked concerned. "This is not good. She's lost a very large quantity of blood. I think

I've stopped the blood loss, but if we don't get her to a doctor right away, I don't think she'll make it."

Adam looked down at Christine. Just like Matt, he was looking directly into her blue, but now not quite so big, eyes.

Christine turned towards Jenny, who instinctively realised that she wanted to tell her something. Jenny moved forward and placed her ear close to Christine's mouth. None of the others heard what Christine said, and Jenny looked quite perplexed, almost stunned.

Adam exclaimed, "Christine, we need to get you to a doctor right now. You must hang in there."

Christine slowly shook her head as she opened her mouth. This time, her words were for everybody. Her audience struggled to hear the words she slowly spoke, her voice quiet and raspy.

"No, Adam. God will be taking me home shortly."

"No, Christine, don't talk like that! We'll get you to a doctor," Matt pleaded as he squeezed her right hand.

"No, it's okay. I am ready to go now. God is calling me, and my questions have been answered."

"What do you mean, Christine?" Matt was confused by her last statement. He stared into Christine's eyes, which were starting to close.

She struggled to open them slightly as she struggled to reply. "The drive. . . up the hill. . . in the van."

"The drive up the hill – what do you mean?"

"Matt, you shouldn't make her talk. She's very weak, and she'll need all her energy," stressed Jenny.

"It's okay... I must tell you before I leave. The third reading – now I understand."

"The third reading?" enquired Matt, now desperate to know what it was.

Christine's eyes remained closed as she struggled to inhale the breath she needed to answer Matt. Her breathing sounded like gurgling water. Christine opened her mouth for a few seconds, but no words came out at first. Finally, she spoke, as if she'd been given one final burst of energy to do what she needed to.

"God cast down his thunder on those who defiled what he had created... Now it all makes sense, all three passages. I have received my forgiveness, and I have found my peace with the Lord. There is just one thing that I must do first. I must pray for you."

Jenny gripped Christine's left hand, the same one that Adam was holding, as Christine uttered her final words. Matt knew she was praying for them, but he couldn't tell what she was saying. Although her lips were moving, the words were too faint to hear. Her eyes remained firmly closed as she mouthed the final words. Matt wasn't sure whether Christine had actually finished her prayer when her mouth finally stopped moving. All he knew was that she had passed away.

Matt felt an inexplicable warm glow travel through his body. It started from his hand that was still holding Christine's, then moved to the top of his head and down his body to his feet. It was something he'd never felt before and would never experience again. With it came a strange feeling of inner peace. As he began to comprehend Christine's departure, Matt also started to realise that he now had a freedom, a freedom from the hold that he had allowed Christine to have over him all these years. Matt looked up at Adam for a few moments, and Adam stared back. Neither had to say anything: they both knew exactly what the other was thinking. Matt felt the tears start in his eyes. He didn't know if they were tears of joy, sadness or relief.

He felt Nancy's hands on his shoulder and turned to look at her. He had always loved Nancy, and she was a beautiful lady, but he now saw a beauty in her that he'd never been able to see before, one that Christine's hold over him had kept him from seeing. Nancy seemed to know what was going on in Matt's mind, and it was the first time since he'd left her in Pine Ridge that he saw her smile.

Nancy squeezed Matt's shoulders hard before speaking. "Christine had lost too much blood; there was nothing any of us could have done for her, and it was too late to get her to a doctor. I know what you all are going through now, but we must clear our heads and be aware of the situation that we're in. We have to get away from here. It won't be long before both Carter's men and the agency will be on our tails. We need to leave now. I'm sorry, but we must pull ourselves together; the consequences of either group finding us would be disastrous. Do you all understand?"

Jenny let go of Christine's hand and placed her hands on Adam's shoulders, before speaking. "Nancy is right; we need to get out of here."

"No," replied Adam. "They're only after me and Matt. Neither group should know about you or Nancy. We need to split up, and you two will be safe if we can lead them away."

"Adam's right," replied Matt. "You two must get away from us." He turned towards Nancy. "Take Jenny. The two of you must get to safety."

"I'm not going anywhere," replied Nancy, abruptly. "And I'm not leaving you, either, John – or should I say Matt. How long do you think it will take for the agency to realise I'm involved in all this. Jenny must go on her own; she's the only person who can't be connected to what has happened here. I'll wipe her prints off the gun."

"Hang on! I'm not going anywhere, either. Jean Michelle and Louise are gone; you guys are the only family I have. Please listen to what I have to say. It's what I was going to tell you when we had our celebration under the steps. There is nothing left for me in France, so before coming back here, I sold everything – the house, my car, even most of my possessions. I transferred the money across to a stateside bank. I was going to buy a house and settle back in America, but I didn't know where that was going to be. I'd left my options open depending on what happened after our rendezvous. I can access that money as soon as the banks open. It's not a lot, but if I can get it before they realise that I was involved in this, it will be enough to give us a start in a new life. Don't you dare try to talk me out of it! It's my final decision, and I'm coming with you whether you like it or not."

Although Adam was concerned for Jenny's safety, he looked very pleased at her decision.

Jenny continued, "When I was hiding in the bushes, I noticed that there was a white Chevy parked behind the house. We need to take that. We can't take the Lincoln; it would draw attention to us. The Chevy should give us the head start we need, at least until we can find another vehicle."

"Okay," replied Nancy. "But we must go now. I'll be able to break into the car and get it started – just one of the tricks I learnt in the agency. You guys get some food, blankets and anything else we might need until we can get ourselves settled."

"And we are taking Christine with us."

Matt's words halted Nancy in her tracks. "Matt, she's dead!"

"I know, but we must bury her with some dignity. There are seven dead people on this property. When the police get here, they'll tear this place apart. When the agency gets hold of this – well, if everything that we've been told is true, don't you think they'll take her body, and they won't bury her. She'll be dissected, examined, maybe even cut up and stored. Even if they did bury her, who would be at her funeral? We can't let that happen; we must bury her."

Adam backed up Matt's words. "Matt said just what I was thinking. We cannot leave her here. We must find a secluded spot, somewhere we can bury her where she won't be found. It's the least that we can do for her, and that's final!"

"I'm sorry, Nancy, but they're right. I can't let that happen to Christine, either."

Nancy reluctantly agreed, despite knowing that the time spent burying Christine would be time better spent getting as far away as they could. Matt did his best to help Adam wrap Christine in several blankets and sheets that they found in the laundry cupboard. Since the arrival of Carter and his acquaintances, the adrenalin had masked Matt's pain, but now he felt everything catching up with him, and he had to contend with just watching though his now blurry vision as Adam carefully placed Christine's body into the trunk of the white Chevy Impala. Nancy had managed to start the car, which to her relief had a reasonable amount of gas. With food, containers of water and a few other items, including a couple of shovels that Adam had found in the garage, now loaded in the car, Adam positioned himself in the driver's seat.

"I'll drive, for the first part, anyway. You might need to keep an eye on Matt; check that he doesn't start talking incoherently," he said to Nancy.

"Sounds like the best idea. Jenny, you get in the front, and we'll get in the back. I'll be glad to get some rest myself."

Adam put the car into gear and proceeded to the bottom of the driveway. He brought the car to a stop at the intersection with the road before turning to Matt.

"Which way, buddy – left or right?" Adam asked, although not sure whether Matt would be fit to give a well-reasoned answer.

Matt looked groggy and a bit puzzled but answered Adam's question. "I don't know where we are; I don't know what county we're in. I don't even know if we're still in Ohio, but I think we should turn left."

"Okay," replied Adam, "Left it is." Adam put the car back into gear and pressed down on the accelerator, causing a small cloud of dust to spin off the back wheels as the accelerating car moved from the gravel to the road surface.

Chapter 16

September 1997

It was a surprisingly cool afternoon as Cecilia Gibbons walked briskly down the main road of the small town of Riverose. She was trying to be as discreet as possible and took every opportunity that she could, without being too obvious, to stop and check she was not being followed. A couple of quick stops outside the windows of some local shops allowed her to check the people around her, and specifically to check that none of them was following her. When fully convinced that she was safe, Cecilia proceeded to the Post Office, or more correctly, the phone box outside it. From there, she intended to make the phone call that was imperative for the safety of her friend and ex-lover. Her hands shook as she slowly deposited the coins into the payphone, the glass back of the phone compartment helped her get a last reflective glimpse to reassure herself that nobody was watching. Slowly, she dialled the out-of-state number she knew well and prayed would be answered.

"Damn you, answer!" The words rolled quietly off her breath as the phone continued to ring, but there was no answer. Unfortunately, there was no answering machine to leave a message on, either, although even if there had been, she would have been reluctant to leave one. Cecilia replaced the hand piece slowly back on the phone. She would have to try again later if the opportunity presented itself, but she also realised she needed a secondary plan in case, like now, there was no reply. She was also aware that she may not actually have an opportunity to make a second call from the public phone, and making a call from the hotel room would be far too dangerous.

Cecilia agonised about sending the letter. She was concerned that it might not get to the intended recipient in time, or worse still, it might get intercepted. However, it was a chance she had to take. The letter was short and cryptic, but the recipient would surely know what she meant and heed the warnings of possible impending danger. There was also no time to write any sentimental sloppy bits. With the letter sealed and stamped, she placed it in the letterbox, glimpsing at the collection time, which indicated the mailbox should be cleared in less than half an hour. She prayed that the letter would find its intended reader safely, and then she continued her brisk walk.

Chapter 17

1997 had been a good year for logging. It was mid-September, and the logging crews working the Frazer Mountains were making the most of the ideal conditions before the rains came.

For Jerry Pitcher, it had been just another day. It was hard work but because he was being paid per tree, he was making the most of the opportunity to earn extra cash. Today, however, a relatively early finish was compulsory for the crews as two logging machines were down and it was now the mechanics working the extra hours, getting them sorted for the next day's catch-up. The earlier-than-normal finish meant Jerry was looking forward to the cold beer calling out to him from his fridge. Jerry's wife, Anna, wasn't due home for at least another hour, so it would also be a good opportunity to surprise her by getting dinner ready. Perhaps it might even end up being a romantic evening. Maybe a Barry White record playing as she walked in would be a good clue to what he had planned for her. Jerry smiled to himself as he started preparing the evening meal.

The phone rang two times and two times only. Jerry's heart skipped a beat as he looked at his watch to check the exact time. If the phone was to ring in exactly another two minutes, then he would know who'd be at the other end. Were the two rings purely coincidental? Perhaps a wrong number. Or would it be a call that would require a level of secrecy? Drawing together his thoughts, he slowly paced around the house, peering at the hands on his watch as they slowly ate away the time. The anticipation was tense, and despite expecting it, his heart once again skipped a beat when the phone rang a second time, precisely on cue.

The voice at the other end sounded nervous as it asked the pre-planned question. "Is Harry there, please?"

An answer from Jerry of "Sorry, you have the wrong number," would have been an indication to the caller that the line was not secure.

However, Jerry knew he was the only one at home and he had no reason to believe that anybody was listening in on the call, so he gave the answer to indicate that everything was okay. "I'm sorry, but Harry isn't here at the moment. Can I leave a message?"

Both the caller and the recipient now knew that their conversation was safe, and it was okay to proceed.

Anna was pleasantly surprised to see that Jerry was home early, but she knew immediately that something was wrong when she walked through the door. The dinner was cooking on the stove top, but Jerry was sitting quietly, blankly staring out the window towards the distant mountains.

"What's wrong, honey?" It was a question that didn't get an immediate answer.

Instead, Jerry turned around slowly to look her in the eye. "Adam rang, and Jenny is missing. It appears that their identities and maybe ours may have been discovered. We could all be in trouble."

The look of horror on Anna's face was apparent as she brought her hands up to partly cover her mouth. "Holy shit! Where is she? What has happened?"

"He wouldn't say too much except that he had to leave the house and is on the run. He wanted to let us know so we could decide what we want to do."

"What do you mean by that, Matt?"

It had been a long time since either of them had referred to the other by their true name. As far as anybody in their new life was concerned, they were Jerry and Anna Pitcher from California. However, at this point in time, it really didn't seem to matter.

"I mean that he's given us the option of going with him to find Jenny or staying here and trying to continue with our new life."

"I am sick of being on the run, Matt. I'm not a criminal, yet we've been living the lives of fugitives. I know that I can never be Nancy again. First, I had to be Clare, and now Anna. Damn you, Matt, and damn your friends. I don't know who the hell I am any more or who else I am going to end up being. I thought it was finally all over. Adam can go look for her, but we have our own lives. We can't keep this up; you'll have to tell him that we can't help. I'm sorry, Matt, but that's final. It's not our problem!"

The bedroom door slammed heavily. Matt could hear Nancy sobbing, and he knew from experience that it would be best to give her about fifteen minutes before he followed her into the room.

He waited before gently knocking on the door and turning the handle.

"I'm afraid it's not that simple," he said. "Adam received a letter from Jenny warning him that her cover may have been blown and that she was more than likely being followed. She didn't know how much the authorities knew about her, but if she's been apprehended and identified, they would have been able to track her to Adam's address. She warned him to leave and not return. He didn't know if anybody knows about us; we may or may not be in danger. The worst-case scenario as I see it, and I am praying that it isn't the case, would be that Jenny has been captured and someone, whoever they are, has extracted enough information out of her to put us all in danger."

"But we might not be in danger. We could possibly live out our lives together happily here and never be found out. You, of all people, know how long it's taken us to get our new lives and new identities together. We both have good jobs, and we have each other. We can't risk losing everything! I'm so sick of running. I just want a normal life."

"I fully understand what you're saying, but we could be in danger even as we speak. Someone might find out who we really are, and I'm not willing to take that chance. Also... well, Adam's–"

"Adam's what? What's the matter?"

"He's like a brother. No, he *is* a brother, and Jenny is a sister. I can't let them down."

"And I supposed you saw Christine as just a sister as well!"

Matt knew exactly what Nancy was alluding to. It wasn't the first time that Christine's name had been brought up with jealous undertones. But he chose, as he normally did, to ignore the comment. Surely she could see the gravity of the big picture. Jealousy seemed so childish when their lives could be at risk.

"You grew up with a real family. I didn't. Adam and Jenny might not be blood relatives, but they are my family!"

As much as she hated to admit it, Nancy realised that Matt's mind was well and truly made up. As far as Matt was concerned, they were his family. She also realised that Matt was probably right about the danger of staying. If Jenny had been apprehended, they were all faced with a dangerous dilemma, and there was no guarantee that they could safely stay here as Jerry and Anna. The hope she'd had for the future was gone. The reality of the whole situation was that they were on the run and always would be for the rest of their natural lives.

Letting her husband go by himself was not realistic, so that left her only one option: join him and hopefully find their friend Jenny.

"Okay, where do we meet him? If he's had to leave his home, I guess it's one of the places we agreed to in the event of an emergency."

"The lake." Matt looked at Nancy to confirm she was willing to come with him.

Nancy knew exactly what Matt was thinking, and she smiled. It wasn't a deep loving smile, but it was still a smile. "I really don't have any choice, do I? You know, I am really going to miss this place. I could have happily grown old here; being Anna wasn't too bad, actually. But if we have to go, then we'd better go as soon as we can. It's a long drive, and I guess we shouldn't hang around here any longer than we have to. You'd better get dinner finished quickly; it's going to be a long night. And we'd better make the calls, then. I guess we'll be sticking to the same story we agreed on in a case like this?"

Matt nodded as Nancy spoke the story aloud.

"Okay, then – my mother, Betty, has just been given days to live, and I need to go back to California to see her. You'll be coming with me as we don't know how long we'll be away. You make your calls first while I compose myself for the full story, then we'd better start packing."

"Remember, all personal stuff but nothing big, and we'd better check that all the documents are in the departure bag."

The departure bag Matt referred to was one where they kept all their important papers, allowing them to be grabbed at a moment's notice. They knew that in an emergency, even if they took nothing else, as long as they had the bag, their tracks were covered. They could access what little money they had left, and they had all the documentation to start a new life.

Nancy nodded as tears rolled down her cheeks; she slowly walked into the bedroom. Matt lifted the receiver and made the two calls he'd hoped he would never have to make again. The first to his employer, and the second to their landlord. Both calls were similar, informing the recipients that they'd received a call to say Anna's mum was terminally ill, and they were heading back to be with her for an unspecified length of time. They hoped it was a plausible story that would not arouse suspicion and would permit them a safe getaway. Matt pulled off both calls like an expert, leaving no question of his sincerity. He also informed their landlord that the rent would be deposited on the first of the following month as normal. The genuinely sympathetic response from both men left Matt feeling guilty – family tragedies were something that should never be lied about, but these were exceptional circumstances. Now it was time for Nancy to make her calls.

Returning from the bedroom, Nancy took a deep breath before taking the receiver from Matt.

Chapter 18

The south-easterly drive had taken them through the long cold night, and arriving at the lake now bought feelings of both relief and fear. The early-morning lake surface was still and extremely beautiful, with the hills and trees reflected in an almost mirror image. A cloud of dust followed the white Toyota as it made its way along the gravel road, finally stopping adjacent to the river in a small parking area.

Matt turned off the engine before turning to Nancy. "It's not exactly my first choice for how things would work out."

She nodded and sympathetically replied, "I know, Matt. Let's just get it sorted so we can start our lives all over again."

The minutes turned to hours as the sky slowly got lighter. The deafening silence was a stark reminder of the remote location. Although he'd not said anything to his wife, Matt was starting to wonder whether being there was actually a good idea. A collection of thoughts, most of which he'd been repressing, made their way into his mind. What if Adam had been caught and had divulged this location? What if Adam knew he was being followed and was never able to make the meeting because he didn't want anyone to get to them? Should they run? Or maybe just go back to their new life after a few days? Consequently, explaining their quicker than expected return was due to Anna's mum's sooner than expected passing, in the hope of not arousing suspicion. As beautiful as the location was, neither Matt nor Nancy were prepared or looked forward to spending any more time in their car. Finally, something caught the Matt's attention from the corner of his eye as a beam of light shone from the adjacent trees. He sat up abruptly.

"Well, that's either Adam or it's trouble. Either way, I have to find out."

Nancy reached for the .22 pistol that was in her handbag and placed it in the large pocket of her coat, before following Matt out of the car and heading towards the place where the light had originated. The pistol gave her a false sense of security; Nancy knew from her training that this was all just so wrong. They weren't in control of the situation; there could be numerous firearms trained on her and they would be none the wiser.

Suddenly, a familiar voice spoke loudly. "Sorry about the late arrival. I had to make sure you weren't followed and that no one had followed me."

The voice from the trees was unmistakably Adam's. The branches rustled as he stepped forward into what remained of the fading evening light. The two men moved forward towards each other a little quicker before embracing in a loving, brotherly hug.

"I wasn't sure if you would actually come."

"We're family, Adam. And we're here for you. So what the hell has happened to Jenny?"

Adam walked back with Matt and Nancy to their car, and as they walked, he began to reveal what had happened since the last time the four friends had met up.

Jenny and Adam's relationship had been rocky: for a couple who had almost grown up as brother and sister, the transition to lovers was very strange in ways and not without problems. However, a unique set of circumstances had brought them together and made them realise the love and respect they had for each other. The events of New Year's Day 1991, now over six and half years earlier, had taken their toll on Jenny. She was tougher than most of the boys she'd grown up with, but despite everything that had happened leading up to the final events of that fateful night, Jenny had struggled to accept that she had taken the lives of five men, including the man who had brought them up, even though her actions had saved her friends. The repercussions of it all weighed heavily on her conscience, and as a consequence, it had slowly taken a heavy toll.

The death of Christine also continued to play out in Jenny's mind. The words that Christine had whispered into Jenny's ear just before her death were words that

Jenny would never repeat to anybody, not even Adam. However, they'd had a dramatic effect on her life.

Jenny and Adam had parted numerous times, and unfortunately, their times apart had become more frequent, but they always got back together. This time, however, Adam knew it was different.

Jenny had left a hand-scribbled note informing Adam that there was something in her life that had to be sorted out before she could ever be the person that she wanted to be, or needed to be, in order to have a normal life with him. The note ended by wishing Adam well.

Adam explained that despite the content of the note, he'd hoped it was just another temporary parting; however, the arrival of the letter confirmed his worst fears. Although cryptic, the letter gave the worst possible news. Adam had to read it several times to work out exactly what Jenny was alluding to, but once deciphered, it informed him that Jenny's new identity was possibly compromised and she feared for Adam, who could be tracked down through her, along with possibly even Matt and Nancy. Jenny apologised profusely but stressed that Adam should not try to find her. Rather, he should leave the house and the life that they had made to once again disappear. The letter finished with something that was obviously about Christine, although it did not mention her directly. Adam deduced it had something to do with her grave. He explained to his friends that he had no choice but to try to find Jenny. The only thing he knew was that she must have been at the site where they'd buried Christine. It was the only lead he had, so that was where he was heading.

Matt totally agreed. They had to head to the small town of Riverose, a place neither of them had ever wanted to return to.

"You need to ditch your car here as planned, then, and come with us."

Matt and Adam had made several plans for possible scenarios that might have cropped up over the interceding years. One of these was to dispose of any vehicle that could be linked to either of them. The lake where they now found themselves was the place of choice for this, due to its remote location and steep drop-off to a great depth. They had also devised a plan for how to sink a vehicle quickly, with minimal signs like escaping air, fuel or oil and without any items escaping or floating to the surface.

"No, Matt. I'm not going to put you guys at risk by being with you in your car. Thanks for your concern for me and for Jenny, but I think travelling in your car is totally stupid if they have discovered who we all are. Dumping the car may have been the original plan, after all that's why we said here. But I was soul searching on the way over, and I will not put you guys at risk. So here is what is going to happen."

Adam's voice was very stern, and Matt realised that he had totally made up his mind.

"I've bought three cell phones; each one has the numbers of the other two already programmed in. I really want to go first, but if they are expecting me, then my presence in town could put you both in danger. Rather, if you agree, I think the two of you should travel ahead. I'll lay low for twenty-four hours and then follow. That will hopefully give you a lead on Jenny before I arrive. If I can, I will try to get another car on the way, but that could present more problems, so don't count on it. I won't phone. I'll wait till I get the all-clear or any updates from you. If I don't hear anything by the time I get to the outskirts of town, I won't enter the area or call either of you; instead, I'll wait another twenty-four hours then decide what I will do. Even if all appears safe, we won't meet in town; if we pass on the street, I won't acknowledge either of you. If you find or see Jenny, I will leave it up to you what to do, but I will not let you do anything that will put your lives at risk. If you don't feel safe, then don't go into the town, or leave immediately if you're already there. As for talking on the phone, I assume you still remember the chocolate banana?"

"Of course, how could I forget?"

Matt smiled; the chocolate banana was a game they'd played when they were small, with certain words having a secondary, coded meaning.

It was another twenty minutes before all the remaining details were exchanged. The three friends hugged closely as a voice in both Adam's and Matt's heads said this could be the last time they ever saw each other. Now, it was time to go. Matt and Nancy drove silently into the night as Adam made his way back to where he had hidden his car.

Chapter 19

Six days earlier, Cecilia Gibbons' red Honda had followed the winding road that hugged the tree-lined river. She knew this was a place she had to return to; a place she had not been to in the preceding six-and-a-half years, and a place she had dreamt about constantly. Being here was going to be part of the healing process, and it was one of three things that she had to do.

Cecilia bought her car to a stop in an area on the side of the road. It was a quiet spot close to the river. She looked at the sign pointing to Paul Lodge, its entrance barred by two, large, distinct wrought-iron gates. Each turn in the road up to that point had seemed so similar, but now she knew that her destination was just around the next left-hand curve.

The sign's red border made it stand out from the green of the trees. The centre part was white, forming the background for the black letters that read, *Wolf Bend Boardwalk and River Cruises*. An arrow underneath pointed towards the adjacent river. Cecilia brought her car to a stop just before the turnoff. *Surely not*, she thought to herself as she took bearings of the surrounding landmarks before exiting the Honda.

It was a few years past now, that terrifying and emotional night. The events that had played out could have wreaked havoc with a person's memory, but Cecilia knew this had to be the place. A sense of fear suddenly gripped her body as she jumped back into the car and quickly made the left-hand turn that the preceding sign had referenced. It was only about three hundred feet from the sign to the car parking area that had been cut into the thick stand of trees. Despite the short distance, the curved access and surrounding foliage made the area quite secluded. The car lot had parking for approximately thirty vehicles. At its extreme end, a boardwalk led to and then followed the riverbank. Adjoining the boardwalk was a walkway that led to a small jetty. A sign on the walkway gave information about the river cruises that left from the jetty.

Cecilia was now beginning to doubt herself. *No, I must have gotten it wrong. This surely can't be the place; surely not!*

A lady returned the smile as Cecilia made eye contact with her and her two young children. "Beautiful day, isn't it! The ferry will be back in about half an hour if you were looking to take a cruise," the lady informed her.

Cecilia replied, "Oh, thanks, but I'm just passing through. This is certainly a beautiful location."

"It certainly is. It's made our corner of the river a place to come and visit, and it's put quite a bit of extra money into the local economy, but they'll need to make the car park bigger."

"Oh. There seems to be quite a few empty parking spots today."

"Yes, but some days, especially on the weekends, there's just not enough parking. I've seen people drive in and just drive off again. They are looking at enlarging the car park. I just hope we don't find any more buried bodies."

Cecilia's heart skipped a beat as she struggled to get her words out. "What do you mean?"

"It was the town scandal at the time. They were digging up the area to build the car park when they unearthed a woman's body. No one knew who she was, but it caused a big fuss. The whole area was completely sealed off, and a lot of out-of-town folks were here. It was quite a big fuss, really."

"Mummy, can we get the ice cream now?" The young boy pulled heavily on his mother's arm.

"Look, I'm sorry, but I'd better go. It was nice talking. There's more about it at the local library if you're interested." The woman smiled once again as she was led away by her hungry children.

Cecilia just nodded, she couldn't get any words out of her mouth, and she remained motionless right up to the point when the lady's car was driving away. *Surely not; it just couldn't be! Of all the places to build a car park, maybe this really wasn't the location.* A multitude of thoughts filled her mind, but Cecilia knew that she had to find out without a shadow of a doubt what had happened. *'There's more about it in the local library',* the woman's final words echoed through her head.

The library, which doubled as the town's information centre and crèche, was not hard to find. It was a very welcoming building with the information centre/book check-out and check-in immediately inside the self-opening doors. The desk held a vertical stand full of pamphlets about the town and the surrounding area. A separate display advertising the river cruises was positioned immediately to its left.

"Hello, can I help you?" The plump, middle-aged lady behind the counter presented a big smile that almost cracked the thick application of makeup adorning her face. A name badge pinned to her more than adequate bosom identified her as Zelda.

"Err, yes. I was passing through and stopped at the river. I just wanted to find out more about the river cruises."

"Well, the times vary during the week, but today, actually, the next one leaves shortly. If you hurry, you might just make it in time."

"Thanks, but I don't feel like rushing. Maybe the next time I'm passing through."

"Well, then, take a brochure. It'll tell you everything you need to know. But there is more to our district than just the river. In fact, you can. . ."

Zelda's speech must have lasted fifteen minutes as she paused only to catch her breath. Not only was she the town librarian and information centre host, but she was also the town gossip. It was quite clear that she knew everything about everyone in town, including all the personal scandals. Cecilia was quite intrigued by everything she, a stranger, was being told, items of a sensitive nature. However, that was not why she was there. What she really wanted to find out about was the body in the car park, and she could contain herself no longer.

"I hear there was a body discovered in the car park. Where can I find out more about that?"

Zelda looked perplexed at the request.

"Oh, I'm a crime writer, and I find inspiration from things like that." Cecilia thought her spur-of-the-moment lie was quite well executed. It certainly turned Zelda's frown into a smile.

"Dear, you should have said! Here I am, talking about things that are of no interest to you. Have a look over there."

She pointed to the two microfiche readers on the adjacent wall, complete with a row of cartridges sitting on a shelf behind the machines.

"Each reel is six months of the *Matheson County Tribune*. Go to the one that covers April of ninety-four; you won't miss it. Looking is free, but it's ten cents for each page you want to print."

Zelda was correct, the discovery of the body and its consequences, including the delays to the construction of the waterfront complex, dominated the local newspaper for several days until all reference to it suddenly stopped. The reels didn't provide any clue as to the identity of the body. But Cecilia feared the worst.

The time taken at the library was longer than Cecilia had expected, as she became totally immersed in the newspaper articles.

Zelda's voice suddenly startled her. "We will be closing in ten minutes; I hope you found what you were looking for."

Cecilia acknowledged Zelda's comment, now realising that time had got away from her, and her schedule was totally thrown. She was tired, hungry and the shock of what she'd discovered had taken a toll. Consequently, the thought of continuing her journey without food or sleep was all just a bit too much. Cecilia had seen all she needed; there would be no further clues from the newspapers.

"Thank you for your help, Zelda. Is there somewhere I can stay the night that is clean and cheap?"

Zelda nodded enthusiastically before recommending the Blue Diamond Motel. Hearing from Zelda that the Blue Diamond also had room service meals made the establishment sound even more appealing.

Cecilia had no problem locating the building. It was well advertised and looked clean from the outside. However, the parking was angular, right off the road, putting all the guests' vehicles on display. Cecilia felt a little uneasy about this. She had her reasons for wanting to keep a very low profile, so it seemed an obvious choice to find somewhere a bit more secluded to park but that was still within walking distance of the motel.

The room was basic, but definitely clean. The double bed, while not the most comfortable Cecilia had ever slept on, would serve its purpose. Cecilia lay down and closed her eyes momentarily as she contemplated what to do next. The emotional toll had left her quite weary. Her rest became a deep sleep, one that possibly would have been a lot longer than the forty minutes it lasted had Cecilia not been awakened by knocking on the motel room's door.

"Afternoon, ma'am." The deep voice startled her as she opened the door to see a man in a police uniform.

"I'm Police Chief Vern Schroder. Have you got some ID, please?"

Cecilia felt a cold chill go down her spine as she fought to gain her composure. "I'm Cecilia Gibbons," she replied, reaching into her handbag for her driver's licence. Chief Schroder studied it for a few moments before passing it back.

"You're a long way from home, Mrs Gibbons." The chief looked Cecilia firmly in the eye.

"Is anything wrong, officer?"

"Not as such, but I would just like a few moments of your time as I heard that you showed some interest in the body that was discovered down by the river a few years ago. Could you tell me why you have an interest, please?"

"Oh, not really taking an interest. I was just fascinated that a body was dug up, I guess. I'm a crime writer – well, not published yet. Do you know who she was?"

"I was actually hoping that you might be able to tell me."

"I'm sorry, but no, I wouldn't have a clue who she was."

"Well, if you do remember or come across anything, here's my number." Chief Schroder looked at Cecilia for a few more moments before passing her a card with his details on it. "And one other thing, Mrs Gibbons – you're obviously staying the night at the motel."

"Err, yes, just one night. I'll be leaving in the morning."

"I'd like to catch up with you before you go tomorrow, after I've checked a few things out. Please don't leave town without stopping at my office first. It's in the middle of the main street. You can't miss it. Don't forget; I'd hate to have to come find you." And with that, he turned and walked away from Cecilia.

"Shit, shit, shit" were the only words that Cecilia was able to get out from under her breath. She knew she was in trouble, as anybody digging too deep into the circumstances in which the driver's licence had been issued would not take long to realise that something wasn't quite right. Cecilia also knew that if she was at risk, so were her best friends. She had to phone the man she loved and warn him. But calling from the motel would be too dangerous. She'd have to go out and find a payphone.

Chapter 20

A knock on the door awakened Cecilia for a second time, but this time, she awoke from a long, restless night's sleep. She tried to collect her thoughts as she looked at her watch.

It's eight thirty; I never sleep this late, she thought to herself, realising she was drenched in sweat. It had truly been a stressful night. The rhythmic knock repeated on the door, causing Cecilia to jump out of bed. She hurriedly put on a skirt and cardigan over her thin nightgown before opening the door. The security chain allowed the door to open approximately two inches, enough of a gap to once again see the imposing figure of Chief Schroder.

"I was going to call into your office before I left," she said.

"I am sure you were. But we need to talk – off the record."

Cecilia looked startled.

"Please, Mrs Gibbons, or whatever your real name is. It's in your best interest. I believe you are in danger, so please, you must trust me. I'll wait outside while you get dressed. There is something important I have to share with you, so please don't be too long."

Cecilia nodded before closing the door slowly and calling out, "Give me ten minutes."

It was probably closer to fifteen minutes before she hurriedly emerged with her single, packed bag and was met by Chief Schroder, who had hastily gotten out of his parked wagon.

"Sorry, I had a quick shower and had to check out of the motel."

"I realise you have your own schedule, so I won't keep you too long, Mrs Gibbons. However, I would like to go down to the river with you. We'll take my wagon. I have my private truck rather than my police vehicle because I think that it is in both our interests that we don't draw too much attention to ourselves."

"I really am in a hurry. I'm not sure if I have the time."

"Mrs Gibbons, I'm afraid that I must insist. We can keep this nice and friendly – something that is in both our interests – or we can take a trip down to the station and do a check on your licence." Cecilia said nothing. "I will take that as a yes, then! Do you want to drop your bag in your car before we go? By the way, which one is your car?"

"No, no I'll bring it with me. I actually parked down a few blocks as I stopped and looked for a place to stay, then I was too tired to fetch it. So you can just drop me back here afterwards."

The short drive to the river was swift with not much traffic around. Very little was said by either party during the drive, and it wasn't until the police chief pulled into the car park that Schroder nervously started the conversation.

"Let me tell you a bit about myself. I'm fifty-seven years old, and I've been a police officer for the last thirty-seven of those years. I've made a career out of reading people: I know when someone is telling the truth and when someone isn't. In fact, body language is a bit of a hobby, so I am damned good at what I do. Now, when I say that you're lying through your teeth, I can say it with one hundred per cent confidence, Mrs Gibbons. If I were to do an in-depth check on your licence, I am quite sure there would be some inconsistencies. Maybe you're not even Cecilia Gibbons, and you know what the other thing I can tell you is? You are bloody scared! I don't know of what or whom; you probably think that you're hiding it well, but believe me, you are not. If I'm right, and I'm sure that I am, I could take you to the station and hold you there until I find out who you really are. However, I don't think that's a good idea, because I suspect that by doing so, I would be putting your life at risk. So, here's the deal, I'll tell you everything I know and why exactly we're here, having this chat in my car and not at the office. In return, you can tell me what you know, because I can't help you if you don't help me. I might be the only friend you have at the moment, so what do you say?"

Chief Schroder waited for Cecilia's acknowledging nod before proceeding.

"Six and three-quarter years ago, on a farm twelve miles out of town, I was called by a concerned neighbour to the scene of a crash where a van was found half submerged in water. On arrival there, we found two bodies inside. Scene examination revealed a third dead body, in front of the farmhouse. The two men in the van appeared to have died as a result of the accident, but the third man had been shot multiple times. Three dead people, Mrs Gibbons. Can you shed any light on what might have happened?"

"Oh, three dead people! Um, no. I don't know anything."

"You seem surprised that there were only three bodies. Were you expecting more?"

"No, of course not. How would I know how many bodies you were going to find? Sorry, I can't help you."

"Really, are you sure about that? You see, a forensic search of the area revealed that there were between four and five other people who had been shot or injured. Someone had also attempted to sterilise parts of the scene. From what we could gather, the van had crashed on the way up the hill. A second vehicle got all the way up the hill, but some of the occupants may have been killed or injured in a shootout. It is my opinion that the vehicles had driven into an ambush because shots had been fired from two different directions. Our investigation found shells in the undergrowth north-west and south-east of where the dead body was found. We also established that at least four guns had been fired, with evidence that shots had been fired from where the vehicle was.

"Now the only people we know anything about or have identified are the driver of the van, a Mexican immigrant by the name of Miguel Santiago, whose cousin was coincidentally the man who looked after the farm. The other person in the van was a Mr Andre Lamont, a one-time aspiring actor of French descent from Louisiana. Mr Lamont was a part-time actor who had done several local commercials in the Louisiana area but never really made the big time. And the third man, the one who was shot, was a Mr Herbert Carlsson; evidently, he had run an orphanage in a small town in Ohio for several years. But he'd gotten into some sort of trouble in the town and had moved away with Miguel, who had worked for him for several years. It was a very strange situation, Mrs. Gibbons. I oversaw the investigation, but for the life of me, I couldn't figure out what the connection was. Maybe a drug deal that went bad? I don't think so! Human trafficking, maybe. But probably not, because it's just too far north of the border. Maybe a gambling debt gone wrong, an ex-lover's revenge or just a random shooting; it could also just be a case of mistaken identity. All options are worth considering when you're looking for a motive, but nothing seemed to add up!

"We collected blood samples in the hope of identifying who else might have been there, including someone who was obviously very badly injured inside the house. Analysis of the scene also determined that some of the people involved may have received injuries from the van crash. There was also evidence to suggest that there were several people inside the van at the time of impact, not to mention the fact we found a number of sets of handcuffs around the crash site. Despite the multiple deaths, it was still a local issue. Well, that is until the results of the blood and tissue samples that we'd collected were returned. That's when all hell broke loose! The next thing I knew, the area was swarming with people from Washington. I'm sure that pressure was put on my superiors to keep me out of what was going on. In fact, I was told that unless I dropped the local investigation, I would be dismissed from my position! I was effectively debriefed and told that I would play no further part in the investigation in any way, and that I and my local officers would be banned from the exclusion area. I didn't know what happened up at that farm, and to this day, I still don't. So, Mrs Gibbons, is there anything you'd like to tell me, or shall I carry on?"

"No, please carry on."

"We were naturally dumbstruck. I knew there was some sort of cover-up and justice had been compromised, but for me, it all became very personal. I have no children of my own, but my nephew, Jimmy, whose guardian I had become after his parents were killed, was an aspiring young man with straight A' grades at school. He was planning to get married to his childhood sweetheart once they both turned twenty-one. Jimmy was a young man who was loved by everybody, but he had one fault. Jimmy always let his curiosity get the better of him.

"It was probably the fact that whatever had happened at Grace's Farm was something so big that it even excluded the local police, but his determination to find out what was happening meant his curiosity took him up there to the scene of the crime that night. The official report said that he had been spotted and, when challenged, had attacked a security agent, who was forced to fire his gun in self-defence. The shot that penetrated his chest, according to the officials, killed him instantly.

"Now, anyone who knew Jimmy would know that would never have happened. He was the last person in the world who would have shown any violence in a situation like that. My enquiries came to nothing; pressure was obviously again put on my superiors, and I was told that unless I dropped my investigation, I would be dismissed from my position and would never again work on any police force. I knew that I had no choice and reluctantly agreed, but I vowed on that day that one way or another, whether in an official or unofficial capacity, I would find those responsible for Jimmy's death and bring them to justice.

"Mrs Gibbons, this is where the story gets even more interesting. Three and a half years later, a local development that had been talked about by some businessmen for nearly ten years was finally given the go-ahead. It was eventually to become the Wolf Bend Boardwalk development and car parking area. The area that I am talking about lies adjacent to the river at Wolf's Landing, exactly where we are, but I'm sure you realised that by now! The consortium of businesspeople had been planning the project for several years, but it had been held up for various reasons. However, once all the legalities were finalised, work started immediately, beginning with the parking area.

"It was during the groundwork that they found the body, an adult female who had been buried a minimum of two and a half years. The woman had been buried fully clothed, and the local doctor determined she had died from internal injuries, which made sense since her clothes were blood soaked. The body had no identification on it. Somebody did not want her identified, and had it not been for one small thing, that might have been the case. But written very faintly in the strap of her bra, and almost missed by us in our initial investigation, was the name Carla Reed. Although the body was far too decomposed to verify either way, because she was fully clothed, we presumed no sexual motives were involved. And with no signs of a bullet wound, I didn't initially make any connection between her and what had happened at the farm three and a half years earlier. Well, that is until we gave her name to the Missing Persons Bureau.

"For the second time, all hell broke loose in our sleepy little town. Before we knew it, the area was cordoned off, and some of the same faces I'd seen the first time around were back in town. The cordon lasted for six days. Traffic was diverted around the area, and many businesses were suffering. All we were told was that it was a matter of national security. The man who told me that was very unconvincing, especially when he told me that the two events were not connected. I can tell you that they were; I just don't know how. So, what the hell is going on? I still don't know, but I will find out, and I will bring Jimmy's murderers to justice. I owe that to Jimmy and his parents.

"After things died down, nobody showed any further interest until you came along and started asking questions about the woman's body. I'd asked Zelda to let me know if anybody ever inquired about what had happened, and she informed me accordingly. Whether through body language, coincidence, gut feeling or a mixture of them, I believe you're the first person who can help me find out what really happened. I also believe that you are scared and desperately need my help. So, Cecilia, I have laid my cards on the table. Now it's your turn! Tell me what you know, and maybe we can work through this mess together."

"I really don't know who or what to trust any more."

"Well I've trusted you. Telling you what I know means I may have put my own career or, worse, my life in danger. So please, for both our sakes, trust me."

"Okay, but not here. I don't feel safe."

"I think you might be right with that statement; do you know anyone who drives a late-model, dark GMC with tinted windows? Because that wagon followed us in and parked behind us, and as yet, no one's gotten out. Maybe I'm being a bit paranoid, but I am going to drive out and down the road just to check if they're following us."

Chief Schroder's wagon slowly left the car park and made a right-hand turn away from the town. Checking his mirrors, he anxiously noted that the GMC had also made the same turn and was approximately a hundred feet behind them.

"I'm not happy with this, Mrs Gibbons. It could be just a coincidence, but I really suspect we're being followed. I'm just going to make a few turns to see what they do. I need to hear what you know, but I also have some other things I must tell you, so I'll keep talking as we drive, just in case something happens and I don't get the opportunity again."

Chapter 21

Matt's Toyota slowly made its way around the winding road. It had been a long time since they'd last been here, and there were only a few landmarks from which he could get his bearings. The area was just north of the township and about four hundred yards past a sign, when approaching from the north, that pointed to a place called Paul Lodge. His heart skipped a beat and his head turned when he saw the sign.

"Yes, Paul Lodge. I saw it, too," commented Nancy.

"It must be just around the next bend."

Despite being advertised by nearby signs, the next bend revealed something that knocked them both off balance. Instead of a barely noticeable, narrow path leading into the wooded area, a wide vehicle entrance now led off the road towards a car park. A large adjacent sign read *Wolf Bend Boardwalk and River Cruises*.

"Holy shit, this can't be the place!" Nancy's words trembled off her lips as Matt brought the car to a stop.

"I bloody hope not, but I think it is! It was definitely around the corner from the Paul Lodge sign, and all this was not here before. Just look; it's all quite new!"

Matt repositioned the car at the side of the driveway before getting out and walking a few feet down the road. He gazed at the hill that rose from the wooded area on the other side.

"Ooh, shit. I remember; once we had buried her, I walked to the road to check all was clear before we left. I also looked up at the hill across the road, just like I am now. I never told you this, but that tree on top of the hill lined up directly behind a power pole, and together, they made the shape of a cross when silhouetted against the night sky. And there they are, right there! This *is* the place! I thought the silhouetted cross was a sign that this was the perfect resting place for her. In reality, we buried her close to, if not right in, that car park; that must have been what upset Jenny. Nancy, what the hell have we done?"

"Now listen, Matt, we don't know if she was discovered or not. It might be okay."

"Well, then, we need to find out for sure and let Adam know. If her body was discovered, then it would have made the local news in some way. We need to find out when all this was built and find any newspapers from around the same time. We'll drive down to the town and see if there is any information about when this was opened."

It had been six-and-a-half years since they had driven through the town of Riverose. Last time, it was early on a cold morning, and there were four of them. It was also a much faster drive, and they were coming from the other direction. This time, it was just the two of them, and the drive was slow as they both scanned the town.

"There, Matt, look. An information centre. They should know about the area."

Matt brought the car to a stop around the corner. "Well, what exactly are we going to say, then?"

"Well, from the sign, we know the river area was developed in 1995, so let's just ask if there are any local newspaper records from around that time. We can say it's for genealogy research!"

Matt balked. "Sorry, what did you say?"

"Genealogy research – you know, finding out about your ancestors. Yep, that should sound convincing. We'll be researching your family history, okay?"

"No, not really. Let's make it your family history," he replied.

"Why my family and not yours? After all, you're the one who grew up in an orphanage"

Matt shrugged his shoulders. "I guess you're more convincing than me, and you can bluff better."

"Okay, a compromise then – *our* family history, brother dearest! I'll do the talking, but I just hope like hell they don't ask too many questions."

With the car parked, they slowly walked inside; two sets of eyes scanned the walls of the information centre, looking for any clues. There was a variety of information to be seen, but it was the display in the centre of the room about Wolf Bend and the River

Cruises that drew their attention. This was not lost on Zelda Smith; she was sitting patiently behind the counter, ready to pounce on anybody who needed to be informed about the area.

She called out to them, "You can book the tour here if you want; the boat leaves every seventy-five minutes."

"Oh... Okay. Thanks, but we're here doing some family history research."

"So, what's your family name, if you don't mind me asking?" she asked cheerily.

"Anderson, Tina Anderson, and this is my brother, Bob."

"Well, Tina, I'm Zelda. I've lived most of my life in this area. The only Andersons I know from around here are Brett and Jill. They live on the south end of town. Does that help?"

Zelda's question caught Nancy off guard. "Err, actually we might not be following the Anderson name specifically. We're actually chasing a lead and wondered if there are any local newspaper records from 1995."

Zelda pointed towards the same two microfiche readers and their corresponding row of cartridges that she had indicated to Jenny only days before. She casually remarked, "1995 was the same year the Riverside was developed and the body was found."

"Body?"

"Yes, it was a woman's body..." Zelda started a ten-minute monologue about the events of the time, including how it spiralled overnight from a local event into something that had national significance, finally finishing with a comment about Jenny.

"There was a woman here last week. She was actually a crime writer and was interested in the case. I guess she got what she needed as she left the next morning. My friend Betty at the Blue Diamond said she checked out early and seemed in a hurry to leave. I guess she had to get back to write her book, and I haven't seen her since. Talking about not seeing some people, Police Chief Schroder hasn't been around for nearly a week. Very strange, if you ask me. Deputy Clark said he had to go away quickly for a family issue back east. You can call it my sixth sense if you like, but I don't believe Deputy Clark! In fact, I never have! He's not from around here. He only joined the local force shortly after all that fuss with the body. Now, don't get me wrong, because I don't like to start gossip, but I think – and this is just between you and me – but I think the police chief has got himself a fancy woman."

Zelda raised her eyebrows disapprovingly as if to emphasise her assumption before she continued with the story. "Now, I did not believe it at first, but Eunice Parker saw his truck driving out of town, and there was a woman in the passenger seat. Eunice said they looked like quite a cosy couple. Can you believe that? At his age! I always knew he's a sly old rascal, but I'm not saying he's a bad man. No, not at all! He loves this town and the people in it. In fact, he's always doing his bit for the local charities and would give you the shirt off his back. I guess he just gets those urges that men get. My ex-husband used to get those urges; I could tell when he was getting them! But Leroy knew how to control himself; he knew better than to expect any of that sort of nonsense from me. Instead, he would go for a long walk in the woods until they went away. Leroy used to spend a lot of time in the woods. He was a good man; God bless his soul.

"Now, as for the chief and his urges – well, if you ask me, there is a lot more to Vern Schroder than meets the eye. But not much in this town gets past me. Anyway, I'd better let you do your research. Each reel is six months of the *Matheson County Tribune*. Go to the one that covers April of ninety-five if you want to read about the body. Looking is free, but it's ten cents for each page that you want to print, just to cover costs. Let me know if there is anything else I can help with."

"Err, yes. Thanks. We'll have a look through the reels."

Matt felt like the life had just been drained out of his body. Turning to Nancy, he noticed that she, too, was not looking her best. Matt realised that his hands were shaking as he put the reel into the reader.

It wasn't until they got back to the car that Matt and Nancy felt free to discuss what had happened during the last forty-five minutes.

"Well, I think we can safely say that Christine was discovered. I just don't want to think how undignified that would have been. I feel sick at the thought. It seemed such a peaceful and restful place for her. How could have we gotten it so wrong?"

"Nobody knew, so don't beat yourself up. Remember, we were all stressed out after what happened. I am surprised any of us could think straight. For me, that whole night was a blur."

"Me, too. I know it was nobody's fault, but even so."

"I couldn't help but notice how the newspaper gave full-page coverage to the discovery, then nothing – absolutely nothing at all. That says a lot about who we are dealing with. We need to let Adam know what happened. If Jenny has left, then there's no point in any of us being here any longer than we absolutely have to be."

A short drive found them at a secluded location, which seemed like a safe place to stop and phone Adam. The phone was answered almost immediately by their anxious friend. Matt relayed the events that had happened since their arrival, whilst Adam listened intently, not saying anything until Matt had finished.

"I have to come there myself, but I don't think it's wise for us to be there at the same time. I have been looking at a map, and there's a town called Coatsville about ten miles south of Riverose. Why don't you two go there and get a motel for the night. Try to get a good night's sleep. I will head down there tomorrow after visiting Riverose, and if I feel it's safe and I haven't been followed, then I'll give you a call and we can meet there and work out what we want to do next."

Neither Matt nor Nancy had a better plan, and the thought of a shower and a good night's sleep at a motel was tempting. They knew they were tired and would be able to think more clearly in the morning, so they agreed to Adam's suggestion.

The town of Coatsville lay on the banks of the same river as Riverose. It had rained heavily overnight, but now, as Matt and Nancy stared out of the window of the motel through the light drizzle, they realised how picturesque and beautiful the area was. A nourishing meal, a hot shower and a reasonably good night's sleep considering the circumstances had left them a lot more refreshed. The world and everything in it seemed a bit surreal; neither had mentioned anything about Christine, Adam or Jenny since waking. It was as if events had reached a point where blocking them out by not talking about them was the best option. They only let the conversation go in the direction of what they saw out of the window. For a short period of time, it was like they were on holiday far, far away from reality. This false tranquillity was broken, however, by the sudden ringing of the cell phone.

"Matt, I hope you got a good night's sleep. Now, listen, I think I know where Jenny is heading."

"Where?"

"I arrived at the parking area aware of what I was going to find, but even so, it was still a shock. I know now what you both must have felt when you realised what had happened. Jenny was on her own when she discovered what happened, and there would be nobody to talk to about it. I believe Jenny was haunted by whatever Christine told her that night. I can only guess what it might have been, but after standing in the car park, I tried to put myself in Jenny's shoes. She had to have closure on something, and I think she believed that she had to first come here to Christine and then to where it all began."

"You mean Mason?"

"Where else?"

"Then we need to go there."

"Matt, wait a minute. I'm halfway there already. I got a couple of hours of sleep in the car last night, and I'm now in a highway diner having a quick bite to eat. I can get a hot shower here, and then I'll be off again. If Jenny is in Mason, I will find her. I realise just how much she means to me, so I'm willing to risk everything to find her. But I won't put you two at risk. Do not come to Mason unless I give you a call. If you don't hear from me within seventy-two hours, then something has gone terribly wrong and you must destroy the phone so it can't be traced. Then go back to your new lives. If things end, live that life and never try to contact us ever again. I'm only asking this because I love you both."

"No, wait, Adam. I–"

"Sorry, Matt. It's my final decision. I'm turning my phone off now before you try to talk me out of it. Remember, seventy-two hours."

With that, the phone went dead. Matt turned to Nancy, who had heard some of the conversation.

"What are we going to do?"

"We need to follow his wishes. If Jenny has left of her own free will, then she has probably gone back to Mason."

"What do you mean 'of her own free will'? We know she left, don't we?"

"That woman in the info centre, Zelda the gossip, said the police chief had gone missing or nobody had heard from him. Her description of his character sounded like someone who would not just do that. What if the woman he was seen leaving with wasn't his girlfriend but was Jenny? The timing would add up, wouldn't it?"

"Well, yes, I guess so. But why would Jenny leave with the police chief?"

"Well, there are only two answers to that question. Either, and I hope this is the case, the chief knows something and he's trying to help Jenny, or he's working for the bad guys and has taken Jenny to someone to extract information about us from her."

"Oh, shit. If you're right, I pray that it's the first scenario."

"Well, if I am right and it's the first scenario, then her car has to still be somewhere in Riverose. I think finding it would confirm my theory. Adam said she was driving a red Honda."

"Right! Let's check out and go back for a look."

Chapter 22

"There, over there! Look, pull over – up ahead."

Matt wasn't sure if Nancy's words brought fear or relief. They had been driving around Riverose for a while and had passed the point where they had both started to feel they might look suspicious. Nancy was quite correct; it was a red Honda Prelude with out-of-state plates, not hidden, but parked in a way that made its presence barely noticeable to someone just driving down the road. After a brief discussion, they decided that Nancy would take a drive down the road and wait whilst Matt walked back and checked out the car. There was no other traffic on the road, and nobody obviously in the vicinity, so now was as good a time as any. Nancy didn't have to ask what Matt's conclusion was on his return. He just looked at her and nodded.

"It still doesn't prove that it was her in the police chief's car, though."

"Well, now that you mention it, I have been thinking. Here I am, acting like a criminal on the run. Well, I'm not a criminal, and I'm not married to one. I am a loyal law-abiding American who always served my country's best interests during my time in the department. If the chief's absence is suspicious for either of the reasons that we suspect, then based on what old nosey knickers was saying, there's a good chance that the deputy is part of the cover-up."

"And what do we do about it?"

"Well, we can find out if the police chief's absence is being covered up."

"Nancy, you are a smart woman. But how are we going to do that?"

"We had a saying in the department: 'It's always easy to bullshit a bullshitter.' I'm going to see this Deputy Clark."

"Nancy, I don't think that's a good idea."

"Trust me, it's time to start being proactive and getting answers rather than hiding like someone on the run."

"But we are on the run."

"The local police won't know that. Walking into a police station would be the last thing that they would expect from someone in our situation. Trust me, and let me do the talking."

Nancy strolled nonchalantly into the police station and addressed the man behind the desk. "Morning. Is Vern Schroeder around?"

"No, ma'am. I'm sorry; he is away. I'm Deputy Sherman Clark. Can I help perhaps?"

"Oh, I'm Tina Anderson, an old family friend from way back, and this is Bob. We were passing through the area and just by chance heard that Vern was the local police chief. I thought I would drop in and say hi as we'll be leaving soon. When he is due back?"

"I'm not sure, ma'am. He has family issues back east; a dying relative, I believe."

"Oh my God! It must be his Aunty Alice. Did he say?"

"Yes, I think that's who he said it was, ma'am."

"I am so sorry to hear that. Can you wish Vern all the best when he gets back and apologise that we couldn't stay, but we're on a tight schedule."

"I will. Thank you, ma'am."

The deputy closed the door behind them as they walked to their car around the corner. Both Matt and Nancy waited till they were a ways down the road before talking.

"Holy shit, Nancy! I can't believe you had the balls to just do that. What if Schroder was around the back or if Clark and that Zelda woman start talking and she tells him that we were here yesterday?"

"I don't think she's exactly a fan of Deputy Clark, so that's unlikely. And anyway, he was on the back foot as he was lying through his teeth. 'Aunty Alice', my ass. I could have used any name or said it was an uncle. He is definitely covering up the chief's disappearance, so I only hope that it's my first scenario, and my gut feeling tells me that it is."

"I know he told me not to call, but I have to let Adam know."

Matt's call went only to the voicemail of a phone that had now been turned off.

"Damn, he did say he was going to turn it off. Well, I need to go, regardless of what he said. But I don't want to put you at risk. You can go back and just say we split up and won't be coming back. You'll be safe and can start over without me."

Nancy was incensed. "I'm offended that you could even suggest something like that! Anyway, we're both up to our necks in it, so sit back, shut up and enjoy the scenery until we swap driving later."

"Adam has quite a few hours on us and could almost be there, and we can't afford to be pulled over for speeding."

"I said shut up and enjoy the scenery."

Matt had known Nancy long enough to know that when she talked like that, the best thing to do was to be quiet and keep a low profile.

Chapter 23

The hours and miles ticked over as their car headed in a north-eastern direction. Matt had decided to make the most of Nancy driving. His eyes were closed, and he was slumped in the passenger seat. His thoughts went back to the time that he was last heading to Mason, over six-and-a-half years earlier. The last time, his thoughts and emotions were that of anticipation and excitement, of reuniting with his friends after such a long time, and of course, his thoughts were on the lovely Christine. This time, he had concern and fear for the safety of his remaining friends.

Nancy had gotten over her annoyance at Matt's comment. In fact, she seemed a bit sheepish, and it had become clear to Matt that she wanted a deep conversation.

"Remember when I told you about my baby? It was definitely not the time or place to have that conversation, but the situation dictated otherwise. Everything that I told you then was true, but there's still the rest of my story that I need to get off my chest. I don't want to be hanging onto any more secrets, frustrations or anger."

"Of course, I remember, and you have my undivided attention."

"After I got back from the sisters' home, I was extremely angry with my parents, and I wanted to hurt them as much as I possibly could. I thought that if my parents' social status and respectability in the town was more important than I was, then that's where I would strike.

"My parents' friends weren't stupid. They must have realised that I'd gone away because I was pregnant. I could have told everyone, but I didn't think it was a good idea for me or my baby. I know she went to good parents who were unable to conceive, so what was done was done. I decided that I should punish my parents by showing their friends what a bad job they did bringing me up.

"I needed to get a reputation, so I started wearing revealing clothing and flirting with any boy who would talk to me. I had some horrendous rows with my parents, and I sure as hell made sure they knew that what I was getting up to was all their fault. To cut a long story short, this very sad chapter of my life finished with Mario. He was an Italian American and on the local football team. Mario was muscular and a very good-looking man. He had the reputation of being a bit of a player, but although he kissed me, he never tried to take advantage of me. I didn't care as long as my parents thought I was destroying the family name. One Sunday evening, I showed up at Mario's house unexpectedly. The back door was unlocked, so I let myself in to surprise him, but I was the one who got the surprise. I heard noises coming from his bedroom. I burst in, and, well, he was in bed with..."

"Someone you knew?" Matt expected Nancy to name of one of her friends.

"No, not exactly. It was another guy from his football team. I was shocked. Why would he choose another man over me? How could I have not seen that coming? I guess, looking back all these years later, the clues were there all along. But stupid, stupid me, I was totally humiliated. My efforts to hurt my parents had backfired. I cut myself off from my friends and lost myself by studying hard to catch up on all the education that I'd missed when I was pregnant at that horrible place."

Matt struggled to comprehend what he was hearing. There had been no previous clues to such negative family issues. Nancy's parents had always been the closest thing to real parents that he'd ever known. "You obviously made amends with your parents; I would never have guessed there was that amount of animosity in the past. Things were always so good between us and them."

"Yes, definitely. It all came to a head one day. My parents told me that making me give up my baby was the biggest mistake they'd ever made. The three of us cried and cried. It was something that needed to happen. They asked for my forgiveness, which I gave them, and it was the start of a process that ended with all our wounds and hurts healed."

"Your parents were just like real parents to me, that's why I felt a little hurt knowing I was excluded from certain aspects of my relationship with them. I guess it makes sense now."

"I was very lucky to get the job at the agency; a family friend worked for them and suggested I apply, as he was able to arrange an interview. Well, three months, three interviews and numerous physical, intellectual and psychological tests later, I was accepted. It was a new chapter in my life. I was only twenty, but I was very keen to learn and impress my superiors."

Nancy's next statement caught Matt totally off guard.

"When we made love that Friday night after the shop closed, I knew it was your first time." Matt was quite embarrassed, but he said nothing. However, even that was not missed by his wife. "It's okay. It was what made it so special for me. You were the first man I truly loved. I never wanted to lose you. I didn't want to give up the agency, but I had to as I could not continue watching you in a professional manner once it was personal. When they didn't assign anyone else, I thought they must have assumed that although I wasn't officially looking after you, I would make sure you kept to your side of the bargain.

"When I realised how you felt about Christine, I was jealous. I had all sorts of bad thoughts. What if every time we had made love, it was her that you were thinking of? What if you had come to the reunion and Christine was the only other one who turned up? Would you have told her about me? Or would the two of you have gone off together? We've both done, thought and said things in the past that were wrong. I would like to think that we are both now mature adults, so how about we apologise to each other and put it all in the past. I will go first. Matt, I am sorry."

"And I am sorry as well, Nancy."

"Thanks, Matt. I feel better already."

There was a pause as they both took a few moments to reflect on what had just happened.

"Now that that's sorted, how about you tell me about growing up in the orphanage. I genuinely want to hear your story."

Since the events of New Year's Eve 1990, Matt had not talked much about his time in Mason, and in all fairness, Nancy had never really asked. Matt had assumed this was because of his early infatuation with Christine and Nancy possibly feeling that she was his second choice. He loved Nancy dearly and had always wanted to bring up the subject of his childhood, but as Nancy was the sort of person who forms her own ideas and sticks to them, he didn't want to do anything that might unintentionally upset her. But now, she actually wanted to hear. Matt opened the subject by clarifying what Nancy had previously alluded to.

"You are right. I was sexually naive."

"Matt, I never said that or meant anything like that. I never loved the man who fathered my baby or anybody else. What we have was, and is, so special."

"But it's true, and I'm embarrassed to admit that I now realise just how naive I was the first time that we made love. I know that I was unworldly in so many other ways as well. Growing up in the orphanage, I guess we all led a sheltered life, but I was happy. Prior to leaving for the military base, the furthest I had been from Mason was a town called Springtown, and that was only a forty-five-minute bus ride.

"I had no appreciation as to how big the world was outside of our county. When we arrived in Cleveland, we were taken aback by its size. But that only eased the shock of how awe-inspiring Chicago was. Growing up in the orphanage, life may have been simple, but it was rewarding. We worked hard and learnt first-hand about appreciating the fruits of your labour. We studied hard and, as a consequence, got good grades, something that was expected of us without question. We also played hard. Sports were fun, and both Adam and I excelled at most sports that we tried.

"Saying that I grew up in an orphanage sounds like a sad, gloomy, loveless experience, but life wasn't like that. We had everything we needed, except maybe one thing: money. Some of the other children at school loved to show us their latest presents and used to hint that, unlike them, we didn't have much. As a young person, it was very hurtful, but as I grew up, I realised that a lot of what they had may have appeared good but was only superficial. I think so many people confuse what they want with what they actually need. I was contented and grateful for what I had. We ate healthy food, a lot of which we grew ourselves, we had good work ethics and we knew the rewards of hard work, camaraderie and friendship.

"I also had a collection of brothers and sisters who were maybe not blood family but were brothers and sisters nevertheless, and it wasn't just the five of us. We had lots of younger pseudo-siblings we watched grow up, and of course, the older ones who, one by one, turned eighteen and left to face the big world outside. We were all in the same life situation, and we always looked after each other."

Nancy had been listening intently but now suddenly interrupted. "Matt, that is what made you the man I fell in love with. You had a quality that other guys didn't have, and now I understand why."

"Thank you. I appreciate you saying that. Life wasn't always a bed of roses; the teasing of the other town children did hurt at times, and there were the occasions when I desperately longed for a mum and dad to hug me and tell me everything would be all right. I used to tell myself that everybody had to have a mother and a father, and although mine might not have been with me, one day, when we die and go to heaven, we would all be together again."

"I am sure that is absolutely correct. You will see them again one day." Nancy found her throat had become dry as she said her words.

"Herbert Carlsson was not the man you met. As a young boy growing up, I remember him as a kind, caring and genuine man whom we all respected. I could never imagine Mr Carlsson as anything but nice, and I still struggle to comprehend how a man like him could turn into an evil monster. I used to think all people were good inside and it was only exceptional external events that could reset our moral compasses. Maybe I was wrong, and nobody is immune from turning into an animal, especially if pushed too far. Maybe even us. After all, Jenny killed five people."

"No, Matt. Jenny did what she had to do in order to save our lives. Some people might be able to turn into monsters, but not everybody. I don't think we could ever become bad; we're just not wired that way."

"I guess you're right, but since seeing Carlsson turn into an evil bastard, every article that I read about murderers has taken on new meaning. I have lost count of the times you see family or friends of killers being interviewed, and you hear, 'He was such a nice quiet boy' or 'She just loved life and other people.' Maybe deep inside, we all have the ability to change and become evil if exposed to the wrong circumstances, no matter how good we believe ourselves to be. But I think that is enough said about that."

Matt hesitated before continuing. This was a time for sharing, but he still had to choose his words carefully. Maybe it would be best to say nothing, but Nancy had opened up fully, so why shouldn't he.

"There is one thing that I feel I missed out on when I was growing up at the orphanage, and I guess the same is true for Adam, too."

"Please tell me."

"This might sound strange, but it was getting to know girls in a boyfriend-girlfriend sort of way. None of the town girls in our school would have been seen going out with a boy from the orphanage, although it was strangely acceptable for a town boy to ask an orphanage girl out. A real double standard there. I remember the school ball of sixty-five, the last one we all went to. Adam and I were in different homeroom classes, and my teacher, Mrs Johnston, considered herself quite a matchmaker. She had organised those who didn't already have someone to take into couples. Well, all except two people, me and Wilma Wang, and yes that was her real name. Wilma was a very large Chinese American girl. She was super smart and always got top grades. I don't want to sound rude, but she wasn't the prettiest of girls, and boy was she big! I told Mrs Johnston that I was going with my friends, but she insisted I ask Wilma, and then, to my horror, she asked Wilma on my behalf – in front of the whole class. I was relieved when Wilma said, 'Absolutely no way,' but I was also hurt and embarrassed because even Wilma Wang had turned me down."

Matt looked over to Nancy to check her reaction before carrying on. "After leaving Mason, there was the military base and then, of course, I met you. Life saw me bypass some of the other things that men would normally do when they are younger, like going out with different girls, going to parties and such; that's why I was so inexperienced when we made love the first time."

Nancy signalled and brought the car to a stop on the side of the road. Turning to Matt, her voice sounded frustrated. "I should never have said anything! What I said was not critical in the slightest. Knowing that I was your first was so special to me. You are a wonderful and considerate lover, and you know just how to please me. A person's sexual experience means nothing at all. Sex is only meaningful in a loving relationship. I bet most people who have had a lot of sexual experience but no real love feel empty inside."

Matt knew he should stop right there as anything further he said would be wrong, but he couldn't control himself or his words. "You're right about love; however, have you ever noticed that when you read an article where someone says sexual experience is not important, it's usually someone who's had lots of lovers? It's like the millionaire banker sitting back in his leather chair sipping his expensive whisky and saying making money isn't really important for happiness. I never really thought about it until I heard Adam's story."

The cold silence made for a very uncomfortable atmosphere in the car, and Matt realised that leaving things at that point was not an option. Starting the conversation afresh was the only way forward. Choosing his words carefully, Matt backtracked to the original subject of growing up in Mason.

Nancy listened intently as Matt continued to talk about Adam, their sporting rivalry, the orphanage staff, Julian and how Jenny used to look after him. Matt was horrified when Nancy noted that he had mentioned everyone and everything except Christine. He took a deep breath and bit his tongue. He had tried so hard to undo the mess that his comments about sexual experience had made, and now he had apparently just made things worse. Nancy's sudden laugh and comments saved him from himself just in time.

"It's okay. I know both you and Adam were totally infatuated with her, but this is now, and as long as we are there for each other, that's all that counts. I, too, have been besotted with certain boys, mainly in my teens, so I guess it's not that different. But thank you for telling me about your time in Mason. . . I have wondered when the right time would present itself, and that time was obviously now. It's just a shame that it's under these circumstances."

Chapter 24

The first sign that made any mention of Mason made Matt's heart skip a beat. Six-and-a-half years earlier, his reaction had been a loud "Yes!" This time, it was a very quiet, "Finally."

Nancy ended up completing the whole drive herself. They had made a couple of coffee and toilet stops during which Matt had offered to take over, but Nancy was still in the driver's seat as their car made the turn onto Main Street in Mason.

"It's a pretty town. I'm looking forward to seeing the orphanage. Have you got a plan now that we're here?"

"I'm looking forward to seeing the orphanage as well. The last time, I couldn't quite figure out what was going on there. But first things first; I'll show you where I want you to park and wait for me."

The memories came flooding back as Matt made the walk that led him to the area under the courtyard steps, an area that was synonymous with sad, happy and frightening thoughts. The area had changed quite a bit since his first time there over thirty-one and a half years earlier. To Matt's relief, the solid wooden door still existed. However, the lock had been replaced with a sliding bolt secured with a large padlock. But while the padlock was in position, it had been cut through. Operating the light switch failed to produce any illumination from the old bulb. But Matt was prepared for the dark interior, having purchased a torch at one of their roadside stops. It wasn't the brightest of torches, but it would provide enough light for what he was hoping to see, and when he saw the bottle of red wine adjacent to five empty plastic cups, it was all he needed to know. Jenny was either here or had been here recently.

"Jenny? Jenny?"

Matt's calls, though not loud, would have been adequate to attract Jenny's attention if she'd been in the area, and there was definitely no reply. Back at the car, Nancy was anxious to find out what had happened.

"How did you get on?"

"She is or has been here, but she's not waiting under the steps, so I have to assume she is still here somewhere, and probably Adam as well. I know Adam. It would have been the first place he looked. One or both of them might be on the lookout as we speak. I think we need to make our presence known without being too obvious."

"I totally agree. We need to get out of the car and have a walk around. We could get spotted by the bad guys, but that's the chance we have to take."

Their first stop was the shops at the centre of Main Street, although due to the lateness of the afternoon, some were already closed. Part of the time, Matt and Nancy walked together, and some of the time, they split up. But regardless, they remained alert, using their peripheral vision to the maximum to keep watch for any signs of danger or of friends. Their next stop was the new town market. It closed earlier than the mainstream shops, but its open layout still allowed people to walk around. Finally, they stopped at the war memorial obelisk on the corner.

"Well, it's getting late. I think we've done all that we can right now," Nancy suggested.

"I guess so. Maybe we should look for a cheap motel, but I really would like to drive past the orphanage, or else I'll be thinking about it all night."

"Sounds good. You can drive; after all, it's your town."

The Carlsson Orphanage – or whatever it was now – still stood proudly. But the now limited light in the sky revealed a building covered in scaffolding. Matt stopped the car and, unable to control his excitement, got out of the car to cross the road. He couldn't see much, but it was something that had to be done.

"We really need to find a motel, Matt. We can drive back tomorrow."

It had been a long day, and Nancy was quite right. If either Jenny or Adam were looking for them, then they had given them plenty of opportunity to do so.

"It's okay. I'm ready to leave."

Turning the car around to head back into town, Matt stopped for one last look at the building, then automatically glanced in his rear-view mirror before pulling onto the road. There was no traffic except for a brown sedan that had just pulled up to park a couple of yards behind them. He turned on his indicator and pulled out.

"Nancy, I'm sure it's nothing, but that brown car could be following us."

Nancy turned around. The faded light and the car's headlights didn't allow its occupants to be seen.

"Make a couple of turns, but don't do anything too erratic," she said.

Matt indicated, first making a right-hand turn, and then, at the next intersection, a sharp left. The brown car continued to follow them, keeping the same distance behind.

"Shit. This isn't good, Nancy. And he's now speeding up to overtake us."

"Okay. Slow down and let him pass. We can't outrun him in this car. If I yell turn, do a one hundred and eighty-degree handbrake turn, and we'll head back towards town. Relax, Matt. It might be all quite harmless."

Despite her reassuring words, Nancy was concerned. She had reached into her bag for her gun as the brown sedan started to pull up alongside them.

"Keep your eyes on the road, Matt. I'll take a discreet look... Holy shit! It's Adam! And Jenny's driving."

Now clearly in view, Adam was indicating with his finger to follow their vehicle before Jenny accelerated to pull in front. Matt followed as the brown car did a series of turns that took it further away from town before finally turning into a narrow lane that led to what appeared to be an abandoned farmhouse. Eventually, the car stopped, allowing a tearful Jenny to jump out of the driver's side and into the arms of her two friends.

"I am so sorry for all the trouble I've caused," she cried out.

"You are alive and okay. That's the main thing. What on earth has happened?"

It was Adam who spoke next. "I told you not to come here till I phoned you. I'm still not sure we're safe here."

"Sorry, but we figured out that Jenny had left town with the police chief, and since you had turned your phone off, we thought we had to warn you. What were we supposed to do? You did leave with the police chief, didn't you, Jenny? So where is he now?"

Jenny looked a bit uncomfortable. "Come inside. I'll tell you everything. I've only told Adam some of what has happened so far. I have a camp burner, so let me make you all some coffee, and I'll start from the beginning.

"Moments before Christine passed away, she whispered something that has haunted me all these years. Up until yesterday, I hadn't told anybody."

"Yesterday?" Adam looked and sounded surprised.

"Yes, I'll come to that. Just bear with me for now. So this is what she said."

Jenny paused for a moment before continuing. "She said, 'Something terrible will happen to my body once I am gone, but do not be afraid as I will finally be home.' Then she said a man's name, 'Colin Macrose'. Most of the remainder of that night is just a blur. I remember her passing away, us driving away with her in the boot then burying her down by the river. I do remember us all saying what a peaceful location it was, and being there again reminded me of how we felt when we drove off. We all knew we had done the right thing for her, so I should have left things there. But I couldn't; her words about something terrible happening to her body haunted me. Why had she told me and nobody else? I tried to console myself with the second part about not being afraid because she would be home. I have never been particularly religious myself, but I knew she was referring to her heaven. Even so, and I know this is going to sound stupid, I couldn't help picturing Mason when I recalled her words.

"Finally, I couldn't bear it any longer. I didn't want to put you guys at risk, so I decided I had to come by myself to visit her grave. Can you imagine my shock when I saw the area was now a car park, and a body had been found there! I didn't know what to do. Originally, I was going to stay the night and leave early in the morning, but when the police chief wanted to catch up, I panicked. Thinking that my cover was blown, I tried to ring you, Adam, but with no answer, I posted that letter, just in case it was my last opportunity.

"The next morning, the chief, Vern Schroder, took me down to the river. He told me what had happened after Christine's body was found and how, as a result, his nephew was killed. He told me everything, putting his own life in danger, and with no one else to talk to, I told him everything except why we were on the run and why they wanted us. I just said it was a military experiment gone wrong. Please believe me when I say I trusted him fully and believed he could help, or I would never have told him, and I didn't tell him where you guys were living. Unfortunately, we were followed. Vern tried to outrun them, and for a while, we thought we'd lost them. Vern told me he suspected his new deputy was in on the conspiracy that obviously went very high in the government, but he also told me about a friend of his in Washington who could help us. He believed his friend knew exactly what was happening but couldn't tell him about it. However, he swore that he could and would protect anybody caught up in the saga. Vern had known his friend since they were boys in Sunday school and assured me his friend was a man of his word.

"We thought we were safe, but the car spotted us. Vern tried and failed to put an emergency call out. We took cover as the car pulled up, and its three occupants started shooting. Vern had passed me his spare gun, and we returned fire. The rest is a blur. I know I hit one of the guys. I don't know if I killed him, but when the shooting stopped, it was just me and Vern. He tried to talk, but he was badly wounded. He just pointed to his car, indicating that I should get out of the area. He then tried to stand up, but he fell over dead."

"Oh God, Jenny! That is terrible! He sounded like such a good man."

"He was, Nancy. He was a good man. I didn't want to leave him there, but what could I do? He was too heavy to move, and I knew it wasn't safe to stay. I took Vern's car and drove close to the main road, where I dumped it, hoping like hell I had wiped off all my prints. I flagged down a passing truck and told the driver I'd been dumped by my boyfriend. It was disgusting what I had to do for him in return for a ride, but he dropped me at a town about eighty miles to the east, where I was able to get the Dodge, as I wasn't going back to Riverose for the Honda. I still feel sick thinking about that truck driver, but I had no choice. There was no one else. He was married, so I am confident he won't be telling anyone about picking me up and where he dropped me off."

Jenny looked visibly sick recalling the events.

"It's okay, Jen. You had to do what you had to do." Adam also felt sick at the thought, but his words and hug were reassuring as Jenny continued.

"I didn't know if it was safe to come to Mason. I was so careful and was sure I was not being followed. I wasn't sure if Adam would even come to Riverose, let alone Mason; after all, I had no way of telling him. I rang again and again, but there was never any reply. I knew exactly where he would look if he came here, so I cut the lock and put the red wine and five empty glasses there, knowing only you and Adam would know its meaning. I decided to give it five days before I came back into town, allowing for the delivery time of the letter. I found this place quite by chance. I would say it's been empty a few years now. I guess it's as safe as anywhere, but there's no power or water, so we wouldn't want to stay too long. But we don't need to now. I have been showering down at the local pool after a swim, of course, so it's not too obvious. And I have been eating things I can heat up on a camp stove. I have some food and bottles of water. I actually spotted Adam quite easily but didn't approach him until I was quite sure that neither of us were being followed. As for you guys, we really didn't expect to see you, and we weren't going to call you. Well, not until we were sure things were safe. Then Adam was going to call you to let you know what had happened.

"I never meant all this to happen. We all had our new lives, I know that. But I had to go back to Riverose and Mason. If not now, it would have been sometime, and as a result, a good man is dead and I have endangered you all. I'm struggling to come to terms with what I've done. Buying the car used up most of my remaining money. I thought there was so much, but it hasn't been cheap being on the run for six-and-a-half years. Maybe it's time to put an end to all this looking-over-our-shoulders business."

"What are you trying to say?"

"I'm not sure, but maybe, just maybe, we should contact Vern Schroder's friend in Washington. It is, of course, up to you all, but I believe there is hope. Vern gave his life for me. I truly believe he would not have given me his friend's name if he were not one hundred per cent sure that he could help us."

"I'm not sure, Jenny. I believe Vern and probably his friend are good men, but this goes so far up the food chain, he might not be powerful enough to help us."

"Maybe you are right, Nancy, but there is something else that I must share with you all. When I left to find Christine's grave, there were three things I knew that I had to do. The first two, I've told you about, but the third was to find Colin Macrose, the name she mentioned to me."

"Did you find him?"

"No. But I had my suspicions as to who he was."

"And who is he, then?"

"Well I was sure that he must have been the pastor that Christine was telling us about. Since I have been here, I've spent a fortune on phone calls, but eventually, I tracked him down and got his number. He now lives in an old folks' home called Spencerville, located just outside Wilkinson, Illinois. After a while, I found the strength to call him. I didn't know what to say except the only thing I said, which was, quote 'Hi, I'm a friend of Carla Reed's,' to which he replied, 'Do not worry, my child. Christine is at peace and with her father.'"

"Wow! Christine must have told him her real name."

"I guess so! It blew me away, but the really weird thing was. . . well, it was just like he was expecting me to call. And when we talked, it was like I was talking to a long-lost friend: he knew so much about me, things that I hadn't told him. With no prompting, he told me there is a time for all things. He quoted a Bible verse about there being a time for everything, then he added that there is also a time for giving up the past and the things we may have done in the past that still haunt us. He then said there was also a time for having faith and for letting go of all the fears about the future. I was totally speechless."

"Holy cow! Did he really say all that?"

"Adam, I would never lie to you. Those were his exact words. Then he said that Christine will always be close, and one day, she wants me to be there with her."

With these words, Jenny burst into tears. Adam held her close again. After a few moments, Jenny was able to compose herself enough to get out the rest of what she wanted to say.

"I must go see him. You guys can do what is best for you, but I know I must go see Colin before making any decisions, especially the one about whether to try contacting Vern's friend."

Adam concurred. "I am beginning to think you're right. Perhaps we should go see this man Colin first. If you two aren't happy, we can give you enough time to get out of here and back to your old lives. As far as anybody is concerned, we don't know where you are and haven't seen you since the beginning of 1991."

Nancy looked at Matt. They were both thinking the same thing, so Nancy spoke for them. "No, Adam, there is a time for everything! I know the verse that Jenny was told by the pastor. We had to learn it by heart in Sunday school. It's the same verse that inspired the song 'Turn, Turn, Turn' by the Byrds. I'm sure you know the line, 'To everything, there is a season, turn, turn, turn. . .'"

"I remember that song, all right. It must've been a hit in late 1965 – I remember hearing it during our final full year in Mason. It was playing regularly around the end of that year and around the time that we made the pact. I know because I can clearly remember that it was the song I was singing in my head when we walked into the area under the courthouse steps." Matt could clearly see the scene as he spoke.

"Wow, now someone's trying to tell us something!"

Nancy continued. "Well, you obviously know the song then, but the actual verse goes something like this, if I can remember it correctly." Nancy coughed to clear her throat before continuing.

To everything there is a season, and a time for every purpose under heaven:

A time to be born, and a time to die; a time to plant, and a time to pick that which was planted.

A time to kill, and a time to heal; a time to pull down, and a time to build up.

A time to cry, and a time to laugh; a time to mourn, and a time to dance.

A time to get, and a time to lose; a time to keep, and a time to cast away.

A time for silence, and a time to speak.

A time to love, and a time to hate, a time for war, and a time for peace.

"I think I might have missed a line or two somewhere, and there is more to it, which unfortunately, I can't remember. The strange thing, though, is that I'm not one for Bible verses, but this is one – in fact, the only one – I remember clearly. I'm not really a person who likes change in my life, but change is inevitable, and when in the past change was forced upon me for various reasons, I found comfort in those words. It reminded me that life is about change, because things can't stay the same forever. Something that is right for now is a different something than was right at a time in the past. There is a time for everything, and just as the pastor said, maybe there is a time for giving up the past and a time for having faith and no fear about the future. I guess I can also add my own line to the reading: maybe there is a time to stop running and a time to embrace opportunities that have presented themselves. Maybe Chief Schroeder didn't die for nothing. Maybe it's all part of God's plan to set us free."

Nancy's words sent a shiver down everybody's backs, including her own.

The four friends hugged tightly. They all knew that, just like New Year's Eve 1990, tomorrow would be a day that would change their lives forever, one way or another. They had two men to meet; they were two men who they had never met before, but they were two men who held the combined destinies of all four of them in their hands. They all knew that it was a time to stop running, but was it to become a time of freedom or incarceration?

Jenny closed her eyes and took a deep breath. A warm, peaceful feeling descended over her, and she knew that whatever may have happened in the past, they were now going to do the right thing.

Chapter 25

Despite the uncomfortable nature of their makeshift bed, Matt realised that he had obviously gone back to sleep after his extended period of being awake during the night. The penetrating cold had the effect of causing his right calf muscle to cramp as he moved his leg backwards, and the resulting pain caused him to quickly stretch his limb straight in an attempt to ease the pain, waking Nancy in the process.

"Matt, what's wrong?"

"It's okay – just a bit of a cramp. I'll be fine."

Although it was cold and still dark, a delicious smell of cooking filled the room. Matt looked at his watch.

"Five thirty! Jenny's up early!"

The anticipation of meeting Colin had woken Jenny at four thirty with a rush of adrenalin that killed any hope of returning to sleep. Looking for an excuse to get up, Jenny told herself that she may not have been able to provide five-star accommodation for her friends, but she could at least give them a nourishing breakfast.

How delicious it was. Adam, Matt and Nancy were all suitably impressed by just how good canned meat, beans and eggs could taste when cooked on a camp stove. Apart from Jenny's early awakening, she and Adam had a good night's sleep, and now breakfast along with strong coffee had prepared them for the long drive ahead.

Sometimes, a night's sleep can put clarity on a hard decision, and this was one of those times. All four friends agreed that seeing Colin was of the utmost priority. Any final decision about contacting Vern's friend, although likely to happen, would be confirmed only by a positive outcome from their meeting with the ex-minister.

"When I spoke to Colin, he said to come along any time as he is always there. He also told me that there was no need to call first, but I think we should. It will be about a six-hour drive, so later, when we've had a coffee and toilet stop, I can find a payphone and let him know that we'll be there in the early afternoon. I don't think it's a good idea to use the cell phone."

"Yes, it wouldn't be right to just turn up without letting him know first. We should get cleaned up and be on the road by just after seven: six hours is a long drive." Matt commented.

"Well, let's get going. I only need five minutes to pack. I'd like to have the time to stop somewhere and have a shower," noted Nancy.

Chapter 26

The aged care facility was little more than a ten-minute drive from the town of Carlton Creek, but it might as well have been half a world away from the small but bustling town. The wooded area that encroached the road leading out of town was in some areas extremely dense, but it had thinned out just before the large iron railings and gates that guarded a gravel driveway. To the outside of the right-hand side gate, a partly faded sign read "Spencerville." The crunching of the gravel under the car tyres gave advance warning of their imminent arrival as the twisting driveway opened onto the forecourt of what was once a magnificent building. From inside their cars, it was obvious to all that time had not been a friend to the building's facade, and with no other vehicles to be seen and no other obvious signs of life, there was a strange sense of emptiness.

"Yes, this is it," announced Jenny to her friends and also to herself, an unprovoked act of reassurance as the four, now-weary travellers made their way to the main entrance.

"You do know what this place is, don't you?"

Nancy's comment caught the other three off guard, causing then to stop in their tracks.

"No, I don't. . . So what is it, then? Apart from being an aged care facility, that is."

"It's an aged facility, all right, but it's also somewhere people send their parents for them to be out of sight and out of the way until the funeral and the divvying up of their assets."

"Being an orphan, I really find that hard to comprehend. I can tell you that having parents is a privilege. If I had my mum and dad, I would want to look after them until they died. How could you want to do anything else?" replied Jenny

"I agree totally, Jenny. I was lucky enough to have grown up with mine. Were they still alive, I would also want to be looking after them. I can imagine how the three of you would appreciate your parents if you had them, but plenty of people only see their parents for what they will be leaving them in their will. I bet the people who live here don't see many visitors."

"Well, their families should be ashamed of themselves."

The solid wooden door seemed to absorb the energy of Adam's knock, giving only a mild muffled sound that did not seem to increase, even though his second knock was significantly harder. With no sign of any response, Jenny turned the door handle, causing the door to move inwards with relative ease. The unmanned reception area directly opposite contained a large polished wooden desk decorated with intricately carved inlay panels. The desk appeared to serve no current purpose other than to support two vases of cream-coloured flowers.

"Hello? Hello?"

Matt's calls rendered no response, prompting the four friends to venture farther inside. Behind the desk, an ornate stairway led to the first floor. Adjacent to the stairwell, two passageways headed to the right and left hallways, each with a multitude of doors leading off them. The only sound came from a room in the left-hand corridor, prompting the four friends to make their way towards its source. It soon became obvious that the sound was from a television set with its volume turned quite high. Matt didn't recognise the program, but it was unmistakably a game show.

"Hello . . . Hello?"

Once again, Matt's call received no response. Stepping into what appeared to be a day room revealed at least thirty reclining chairs that held a selection of grey or balding heads, each facing the television set with varying degrees of concentration. Their entrance into the doorway was noted in the peripheral vision of one elderly resident who turned abruptly. That, in turn, caused a wave of staring faces to turn and stare blankly at those who had entered their world, causing the four friends to feel like objects on display. The sight of not one, but four visitors induced a mesmerising effect on the residents, all of whom appeared to be truly starved of contact with the outside world.

Jenny was just about to speak when a deep strong voice beckoned from behind.

"Welcome, welcome, welcome, my friends."

The tall, slim figure was frail, but his eyes had the glowing radiance of a young child. Taking the weight off his walking stick, the man stood up firm and straight. His eyes moved first to Nancy, before shifting to Jenny and focusing on her. His face lit up as he spoke again.

"I am Colin."

After a few minutes of formalities, Colin guided his guests towards and then along the right-hand corridor to his room. Dark-stained oak panels absorbed some of the limited light, whilst the highly polished linoleum floor caused a faint squeaking sound from both Matt's and Adam's shoes.

"Someday, someone is going to slip on this floor. The staff seem more concerned with cleanliness than safety, not that there is anything wrong with cleanliness. As the old saying goes, it is next to godliness. To be honest, however, there is more chance of somebody getting stuck in the old elevator. Thank the good Lord that I am on the ground floor, and as I see it, I am closer to God's green earth. Why people think heaven is up and hell is down, I really don't know. They are both real places, but up and down – that is just far too simplistic."

Colin finally stopped and gestured towards a partly opened door.

"Here is my room. I am so glad you have come to see me. The money is beginning to run out."

"Do you need money?"

"No, not at all, that is not what I meant. Please come in."

Colin closed the door firmly behind his four visitors.

"I am sorry that there is not much space in my room, but it's usually just me here. I hardly get any visitors, let alone four at the same time! I only have two chairs, so I hope you don't mind sitting on my bed."

Colin beckoned Adam and Matt towards the bottom of his single bed.

"We could talk in the day room, but I think we should be in here as there is a bit more privacy."

"We are fine, thanks, Colin," Jenny reassured him. "It's just good to finally meet you. Christine talked briefly about you and the circumstances surrounding her visit to you all those years ago. Unfortunately, the way things worked out, with the accident, she never got to expand on the details."

"Jenny, during our phone conversation, you never actually told me how she died."

"It was a motor-vehicle accident; she never recovered from her injuries."

Colin nodded sympathetically; Jenny, however, had the feeling that Colin already knew the answer.

"Christine had a beautiful heart," he said quietly. "When she came to see me that cold night, she was looking for answers. Now I suspect the four of you are looking for the same. I hope that I can help you find what you are looking for, just like Christine did. Just to be quite clear, I am not going to try to convert you religiously. If you have views that are different from mine, then I fully respect that, so please, do not feel pressured in any way whatsoever. Anything you choose to do must come from your heart and not because you feel obliged."

Adam felt quite relieved at Colin's assurance.

"Thank you, Colin," he said. "I am not religious in any way whatsoever, but I also respect your views. You were totally correct with the other thing that you said, as we are looking for answers that hopefully you might be able to provide."

"Then I will try to give you just that. I would like to start by telling you a bit about myself, if that's okay. It will help my story to make sense."

The four friends nodded their approvals.

"When I was a boy, I always wanted to be the captain of a big ocean-going liner like you see on television, but by my adolescence, I knew my destiny was to be a pastor. I completed my religious studies with top grades and had a very successful life growing churches and serving God and his people. I guess to most of my flock, I was the 'perfect pastor,' but not so! Unbeknown to everyone else, inside me there was something missing, and it troubled me deeply. I knew it was something that I needed to do, but no matter how much I prayed, I could not identify what it was.

"I would dream regularly of a blonde woman with big blue eyes, but I could never make the connection. In fact, each Sunday, I used to scan the congregation, just in case she had turned up as a visitor. But that was never the case. God had a plan for me, though. I was introduced to the works of Nachmanides. . . but more about him later. This led me to a line of study that, shall we say, is slightly outside the teachings of mainstream theology. However, what I learnt prepared me for that cold, wet June evening many years later when that blonde lady with the big blue eyes finally showed up. I say cold and wet, but that evening, it was strangely hot in my study, so much so that I had opened the door that led onto the courtyard. I had been working for about two hours when I realised that the whole purpose of what God had planned for me was about to happen. My whole body tingled in anticipation for several minutes before I felt the presence of another person, and before even turning around, I knew who she would be."

"Christine."

"Yes, Christine. She was soaked to the skin, but that was the least of her problems. She was spiritually in a very bad place. I got her some dry towels and a hot coffee, and we started talking and talking. Every time I opened my mouth, I didn't have to think about what I was going to say: the right words just came out. They were, of course, not my words but God's. I was able to offer an explanation for everything she said or asked. It was the first time it had happened, and it has never happened since.

"There is much that we talked about that I cannot share with you as I feel it would break the trust she placed in me. However, there are other things I know that I must share with you, particularly about that which is inside you. Would I be correct in saying that this only applies to you two, Adam and Matt?"

The men looked at each other in total disbelief before Matt asked the obvious question. "How do you know there is something inside us?"

"Christine knew there was something inside her that did not belong there, and with God's help, I was able to tell her what it was. We talked and prayed over the situation, and she found the peace that she so longed for. Christine also said she had some friends who could be in the same situation, and she hoped to meet up with them again one day. I think I would be correct in saying those friends would be you?"

"So you're saying that Christine knew they had put something inside her? Well, she couldn't have, because we only found out a few years ago, and she was as surprised as we were. So it just can't be true."

It was not Colin who responded to Adam's statement but, rather, Jenny.

"Adam, Christine did know. I am so sorry. I should have told you."

"What do you mean, Jenny? We didn't know what was going on till the doctor told us, so what have you not told us?"

Jenny suddenly burst into tears; she tried to get her words out as Adam came over to give her a hug. Eventually, she was able to compose herself enough to give an explanation for her statement.

"Christine's last words were very weak; there was something else that she said that I never told you. She said that what you and Matt had inside you needed to be dealt with before you died. She also said that she had already dealt with hers and so had no fear of dying. Christine knew she would not be able to help and asked me to help you both. That responsibility was just too much for me. Every time I tried to bring it up with you, the conversation ended up going in a different direction. Going to Christine's grave was supposed to be a way for me to go and talk to her and hopefully give myself some direction as to what to do. None of us are getting younger; what if you or Matt had died and I hadn't done what I told Christine I would do? How would I live with myself? With us separating from Matt and Nancy, I might never have seen Matt again, anyway. I am so sorry I have let you all down, including Christine."

Jenny continued to sob as Colin stood up and spoke. "Luckily, it's not too late. Matt and Adam, you are both here now. We can sort out what we need to sort out right now. Christine will be happy, and you, Jenny, will have fulfilled your promise to her."

Matt responded. "Thank you, Colin! Is it okay with everybody if I tell Colin what happened when we met Christine in 1990?"

The others nodded, and Matt relayed the events of that cold New Year's morning. Near the end of the story, he wrapped it up. "So that was it, the three of us finding out that we were the victims of some bizarre government experiment where we had alien DNA implanted in us from some crashed spaceship or something. That, in turn, made us different and worth lots of money, which is why, for the last seven years, we have been on the run. And the government department that was running the operation is trying to capture us so they can have their guinea pigs back."

"Actually, Adam, you don't have DNA from some alien race. What you have had implanted in you originated from a source a lot closer to home."

"How would you know? You're not part of their plot... Are you?"

"Goodness no, not at all. But I do believe that I have the knowledge to back up what I have just said."

"Well, where did this genetic material come from, then?"

"God has been preparing me for a long time to share with you what I believe to be the case. However, I fear that what I must tell you could be hard to comprehend, and as such, it may fall on closed minds. Therefore, I ask that you hear me out fully before making judgements. How does that sound?"

"I am happy with that," replied Adam as the others nodded approvingly.

"We live in a world surrounded by things that we just can't make sense of, things that defy logic and physics as we know them. I think I can safely say that everybody over the age of sixteen has either seen or knows someone who has seen a ghost. Every week, intelligent, rational people put their reputations at risk when they report sightings of strange shapes, moving objects or black lines in the sky. Who has never had a case of déjà vu? Or had an event happen that you'd dreamt about the night before? What about waking up to smell the distinctive perfume of a deceased elderly aunt who loved you dearly. All these things, plus so much more, have no rational logic, but they happen to millions of people daily from all walks of life.

"Now let's look at things from a slightly more scientific point of view. Recently, both the United States government and the United Nations have candidly admitted that unidentified flying objects are real, but they have never said or indicated that these objects came from outer space. Did you know that despite all our modern technology orbiting the earth, UFOs have never been spotted outside of the earth's atmosphere?

"So what if I were to suggest that all the things I just talked about, the things that we can't explain, including the objects observed in the sky, actually originate from earth and are with us right now, as we speak? We can't, however, appreciate them, as they are in a different dimension, and it is only when they cross into one of the four dimensions that we can comprehend that we become aware of them."

"That's an interesting theory," Adam interjected. "But how can you prove the existence of something that we can't see or touch, and how then do we fit into this?"

"Bear with me, Adam, and I will tell you exactly how you fit in. And as far as proving what I said, I actually can't prove anything, but I can supply you with information so you can make up your own minds. You might be surprised to hear that modern science has realised that we do, indeed, live in a multidimensional world. Many scientists from a variety of nations are working on this very theory, and the one thing that they definitively can't do is disprove the concept. It may sound like modern technology has entered a whole new realm, but the idea of what I just said is not a new idea at all. In the thirteenth century, a Jewish scholar called Moses Ben Nahman, commonly known as Nachmanides, concluded from his in-depth studies of the first five books of the Bible that God had created ten dimensions but man's break away from God in the garden of Eden left us only able to comprehend four. The book of Genesis tells us that prior to the flood of Noah's time, heavenly beings did cross into our world. If I were to say the world 'Nephilim,' would you know what I meant?"

"Christine briefly told us about them on the night of her death. She was going to tell us more, but it just didn't work out. She did say, however, that we could not be Nephilim because we had human parents."

"And Christine would have been totally correct in saying that. Nephilim are the result of heavenly beings, or fallen angels, if you prefer, intermarrying with humans. The resultant offspring, Nephilim, were known to be large and powerful. Let me quote a passage from Genesis Chapter 6:

When men began to increase in number on the earth and daughters were born to them, the sons of God saw that the daughters were beautiful, and they lay with any of them that they chose. The Nephilim were on earth in those days, and afterwards when the sons of God went to the daughters of men and had children by them, they were the heroes of old, men of renown.

"Nephilim could not have children themselves. Instead, they had what was known as the Elioud, so just like ligers, tigons, coywolves, zebroids and other hybrids in the animal kingdom, they cannot multiply. There are many types of people in the world, but we are all human and all descendants from the bloodline of Adam. Therefore, God will never permit hybrids in mankind.

"Genesis also tells us Nephilim were wiped out during the flood. But some biblical scholars suspect that a few may have survived or that others were created after the earth's re-population. Noted giants like Goliath may have been Nephilim. Moving forward through history, many civilisations talk about giant powerful men. Maybe they were the inspiration for Greek Gods like Hercules. My friends, you are not Nephilim and never will be, but I believe you were used by evil men to try to create something similar, perhaps not with superhuman strength, but with other more subtle positive attributes."

"Colin, let me get this straight," Adam frowned and took a deep breath. "You're trying to tell us that the material inside of us did not originate from another planet but rather from a spiritual being that crossed over into our world from another dimension?"

"Perhaps in a simplified way – yes, Adam, that is exactly what I am saying. When Christine confided in me that she knew there was something inside her that shouldn't be there, I knew exactly what it was. It had always been my destiny to meet and talk with Christine and now the four of you. I could not physically change anything that had been done to her any more than I can change you, Matt and Adam, but what I was able to do was put her at peace with herself and with God. You see, God finds what has been done to you abhorrent, and you need to receive his forgiveness before you die, or it will be too late."

"Why do we need forgiveness? We never asked for this to be done to us," noted Jack.

"God knows that you were unaware what was going on, and thus he does not want you to miss the opportunity to receive the forgiveness you need. He would never allow you to miss the opportunity to receive it, so he has brought you here to the one person that he prepared to help you. I realise this is hard for you to accept; you can call me a crackpot and leave if you choose. If you do, I will be sad that I was not able to help you as it is my God-given destiny, but I won't be offended. The other thing you can do, just like Christine did, is you can give me the opportunity to help you. I have all the time you need."

Colin paused before continuing. He realised that his four visitors were still trying to come to terms with what he had just told them. But he still breathed a sigh of relief as none of them had yet called him a crackpot.

"I cannot help you with or tell you what you should do about contacting the government official you told me about, but if you leave here in a better place than when you arrived, I trust you will be able to make the right decision."

Chapter 27

It was six hours after their arrival at the rest home that the four friends exited the building and walked towards their cars.

"Hop into our car for a few minutes. I guess we'd better have a chat about where to go from here." There was a strange tone to Matt's voice.

Adam and Jenny nodded; although there was not much being verbally exchanged, they knew there was so much to talk about.

As the last of the four doors closed, it was Jenny who started the conversation. "I presume that we are still on track to contact Vern's friend, or has our time with Colin changed anything? What do you think, Adam?"

"Before we make any calls or do anything, can we just backtrack a bit? And can someone tell me what the hell just happened in there? I am still trying to get my head around what he was telling us. Do you guys believe all that he was saying, or am I the only who thinks he has one hell of an imagination? Don't get me wrong; he was a nice man, but all that stuff about living in multiple dimensions. . . really? And as for asking for forgiveness – well, that's just stupid. I didn't ask for this all to happen to me. I am the victim in this situation. You were obviously more receptive to his ideas, weren't you, Matt?"

"Remember back when Christine told us about the night she met Colin, walking down the road lost and in the rain, then how she noticed his open door and the warmth coming out of the room? Her story gave me a shiver down my spine. Now, after meeting him myself, I can understand the impact he had on her life. I think Colin was telling the truth when he said he believed that God had been preparing him for his meeting with Christine, and now us. I don't know what it was, but something happened in there, and I feel different inside, like a weight has come off my shoulders, and I now have a good feeling about the whole situation."

Nancy interjected. "I don't know about the rest of you, but I am tired and hungry. I could really do with a nourishing meal, a hot shower and a good sleep. Tomorrow, we could be making the biggest decision of our lives, and I think we all need clear heads. We passed two motels on the way down, so why don't we check into one, eat a nice meal, have a good sleep, and in the morning, if we're still all happy to make that call, then we can drive here." Nancy pointed to a location on the map that she had just removed from the passenger door compartment. "I was looking at my map on the way down. I reckon it's about a four-hour drive, which should be far enough away to create a safe distance from

Colin. So in the worst-case scenario, he can't be linked to us. The town sits right on a major intersection. If we're not happy with the response, then there are multiple directions in which we can exit the area."

Adam concurred. "I think that's a good idea. I'm sure we'll have clearer heads in the morning."

Matt and Jenny also nodded in approval.

Matt was feeling quite relaxed on returning to their motel room. The meal had been delicious, and both Adam and Jenny were sounding quite optimistic about the future. Matt was now looking forward to a comfortable sleep. However, he had noted an increasing change in Nancy's mindset. Normally, a couple of glasses of wine would have seen Nancy relax, but Matt realised that this evening was different. This time, a couple of glasses of wine had bought out a side of Nancy that was starting to concern him. Matt prepared to redirect her changing mind by striking up a conversation about feelings, something that he would soon regret.

"When we were in that old farmhouse, I was scared. In fact, very scared, not knowing what to do or what Colin would tell us, but now I'm filled with a peace about the whole situation. I know we're making the right decision about contacting the police chief's friend. I realise nothing is guaranteed, and I know we cannot go back to what we had, but maybe, just maybe, we can start fresh without having to look over our shoulders. I have a good feeling about things. What do you think, Nancy?"

"I would really like to think you are right. I'm willing to take a chance because I'm sick and tired of being on the run. I guess whatever will be, will be! You are right, though; we cannot go back to Pine Ridge or the life that we had and lost. In the last seven years, have you ever been tempted to phone the store with a fake voice or just make some enquiries to see if they even still exist?"

"I was tempted many times, but I didn't because I always thought it might be dangerous. What about you?"

"Actually, I did make some enquiries about three years ago, and the store is no more. It closed its doors about two months after we went missing. Everybody was dismissed, and now it is nothing more than history."

"Oh, that's terrible. I feel so bad for the staff."

"You sound surprised, John. . . or Jerry – or should I say Matt. But really, did you not think for one minute that the agency was going to be pissed with you, and I mean really, really pissed!? Remember who financed the business in the first place, and as an ex-employee, I can assure you they are not a charity that is tasked with setting up businesses to provide jobs in small towns. Knowing what I know now, the agency was not a bunch of saints. In fact, quite the opposite, but we had a deal with them, and you were the one who broke that deal and lost us everything. We had a business in a community that loved us. We had good friends and a future. When you walked out, you didn't just walk out on me, you also walked out on Bob and Sue and Larry and Rex and Chad and Sarah and all the other people in Pine Ridge who directly or indirectly depended on us.

"This is how I see the best-case scenario for us," she continued. "Jenny's contact is legit and able to help us. Great! But we would all have to be kept out of sight at a safe location until the whole business with the department is wrapped up and the dust has settled. A year, if we're lucky. . . maybe two, three or even five. We would also be given new identities, so there would be no John and Nancy going back to Pine Ridge and saying 'Hi folks, did you miss us? We've just been on holiday for the last eight or ten years.' And of course, I haven't even mentioned the thugs that the doctor was going to sell you to. Do you think they might be just a little upset about us killing a couple of their men? It is quite possible that, in fact, we would still spend the rest of our lives looking over our shoulders."

Matt reacted defensively. "I didn't walk out on you. I just had to make the reunion. It was the only chance that I would have to see my friends again! I was intending to come straight back. I could have told everyone that I was unwell, and nobody else would have known about the reunion."

"NOBODY WOULD HAVE KNOWN? Are you really that naive? I can understand that you missed your friends, and I'm not saying that they weren't good people. You know how much Adam and Jenny mean to me. But you did walk out on me and our whole life in

Pine Ridge that we can never get back! I am going to sleep in the chair tonight, and while you are alone in the bed, I want you to think about this. If you knew for certain that Christine was not going to make your reunion, would you have gone? Or would you have stayed in Pine Ridge and kept everything as it was? You don't have to tell me your answer, but you need to think about it."

Nancy's piercing words left Matt speechless as she got out of bed and made her way to the adjoining room. Matt said nothing: Nancy's outburst had caught him totally off guard. After their talk in the car, Matt had been under the impression that all animosity had been relegated to the past and in turn replaced with forgiveness. Now, not only did he have to face external events outside of his control, but he could have lost the emotional support of his biggest ally and confidante at a time when mutual support was imperative.

It was six thirty when Nancy knocked on the bedroom door. Matt had been awake for a while, and had in fact been awake for the majority of the night. It seemed quite ironic that they had decided to spend a bit extra for a comfortable night's sleep, and due to their own machinations, they'd had anything but.

"Can I come in?"

Matt took a deep breath as he tried to ascertain from her voice whether Nancy was still upset.

"Of course you can."

"Matt, I'm sorry about last night. It was all just a bit too much with us preparing to make that call today and not knowing what will happen as a result. Then there was what Colin told us. Everything that he said makes perfect sense, and that freaked me out! I was awake for most of the night and had a lot of time to think. I realised that I miss our life in Pine Ridge, so I'm still upset about what happened. However, I can't change anything that has already happened, so I really want us both to put all the bad things in the past once and for all so we can both move forward. After all, these are uncertain times."

"I would like nothing more myself. I would really like to give you an honest answer to your question last night."

"I told you that you didn't need to tell me."

"But I want to, as I have to clear the air. If we are to move forward, we can't have any more secrets or things we hold onto. If I didn't have my life in Pine Ridge with you, I would have gone back to the reunion regardless of who was or was not there, and any resulting consequence would have been a small price to pay. However, the wonderful life we had made the decision to go the hardest dilemma in my life. The year leading up to it was nothing more than torment; I would lie awake for hours wondering if I should stay, or should I go? To be totally honest, if I knew for certain that Christine would not be there – well, I would not have gone. All through my younger years, Adam and I were so competitive for her affections, but to her, we were nothing more than brothers, and she would have never let anything happen between her and Adam or her and me. When I drove to Mason, I had all sorts of silly schoolboy fantasies in my head, but when we all met, I realised they were just fantasies. Time had totally distorted my memory of how things were between the five of us. Even if it had just been me and Christine, as soon as I saw her again, reality would have brought me back to earth, and nothing would have ever happened. I would like to say I wish I'd never gone back to Mason, but I can't. Firstly, I could not have coped knowing that I did not turn up and keep my part of our pact. Secondly, had I not gone, you would have not come after me. Would that have led to Jenny being killed? Perhaps Christine and Adam would be locked away somewhere in a dark room, kept alive only so their blood could be milked. The one thing that I truly wish is that we'd never made the pact in the first place. Things are what they are, and I want to move forward with the woman I truly love – you."

"Thank you for your honesty. You haven't told me anything that I didn't already realise, but hearing you say it helps to make it better. I was, of course, not fully honest with you about my job. Growing up with loving parents, I don't think that I can fully appreciate just how things must have been for you and the others growing up in an orphanage. Let's just put all our mistakes and regrets behind us. Nobody knows when their time is up, so let's move forward together and make the most of each day." She paused and then added, "I know we are going to have an early start, but I think we still have time to make love, if you'd like."

All four friends had been in total agreement that morning, and their drive north had taken just over four hours. Now three nervous observers listened as Jenny made the call from the payphone. Finally, she was put through.

"Hello, is that John McMillan? Hi, John. My name is Jenny, and I'm a friend of Vern Shroder. Vern was an amazing man who died trying to protect me from some corrupt officials. Before he died, Vern said that I should contact you as you might be able to help. . ."

Chapter 28

December 1999

It was just after six on that cool December evening when Jenny's car came to a stop on tree-lined Victoria Road in Northville, Virginia. Checking the house number on the mailbox, she assured herself that this was the home of her friends, Matt and Nancy. There was no mistaking the two figures who appeared in the now open doorway. Getting her bags from the back seat would have to wait; she rushed up to embrace her two friends.

The back gardens of the houses on the south side of Victoria Road sloped downwards, with the continually descending contour flattening out only when it reached Clarence Park, which, at over ten acres, was the largest community recreational facility in the surrounding area. The view from the sunroom at the back of number seventy-eight was almost uninterrupted from the east to the south-west direction. Matt and Nancy's neighbours had assured them that the view promised to be spectacular later that evening, when the New Year's Eve fireworks were scheduled to be lit in Clarence Park. In less than six hours, they would be welcoming in both a new year and a new millennium, for tonight was 31 December 1999.

An open bottle of wine helped to set a relaxing mood as the conversation started to fill in the missing parts of the last two years from the different perspectives of the three friends. Jenny was keen to hear what had happened to Matt and Nancy since they'd last met four months earlier. She was also secretly looking for her friend's assurances that their lives could finally return to a degree of normality after the tragic events of the previous year. Jenny also had some news about her future plans that she wanted to share with her friends, but for that, she needed the right moment. Matt's primary concern was to get reassurance that Jenny's life had settled down after Adam's death in August that year.

"Wow, this view is even better than you described it! You were very lucky to get this place!"

"Yes, we think so, too. It was really a case of being in the right place at the right time. We have a year's lease with the right of renewal, so it gives us a sense of security and normality, an opportunity to settle down and start our new life now that it's finally all over."

"So it really is all over?"

"Yes, Jenny, it is. Every morning, I wake up and ask myself that very question, and sometimes, I still find it hard to accept that I can walk down the street a free man. We both decided that taking the offer of new identities was the best option for a fresh start. It was a hard decision, but we knew that we could not be John and Nancy again. That was in a different life. Jerry and Anna lived in a lifetime of fear and on the run; something that does not exist any more, either, and anyway, those were not our real names, so we had nothing to lose by ditching them. By not returning to being Matt, I have severed any last ties with him, just on the very slim chance that the thugs who were going to kidnap us could locate us again, but that is so unlikely that I don't give it a second thought.

"Jason and Lynda are likeable names, don't you think? I know this sounds silly, but when I look in the mirror, I feel that I look like a Jason. Part of our moving-forward process was to be sure in our hearts that we never wanted to go back to either Pine Ridge or Mason. I spent twenty-five years wanting to return to Mason, and the consequences destroyed the life we had built, but I am glad I did because I would never have gotten to see Adam, Christine or you again. That was also in a different lifetime; now, we are the only two of the original five left, and we both have new lives to look forward to."

"I really do appreciate what you mean by moving on. I'm also at that crossroads, and there is something I want to share with you about my future plans, but a bit later. . . Perhaps after a couple more glasses of wine." Jenny paused for a few moments to collect her thoughts before continuing. "When Adam was shot, I thought my world had ended. If someone had said at the time that some good would come of it, I would have asked them to get out of my sight. But as we know, it was that very tragic event that led to the last of the rogue officials being caught. There was, however, something that I didn't tell you about Adam's last moments with us. When we went to see Colin down in Spencerville, I really did not expect to have the conversation that we did. Adam also found Colin's talk very hard to comprehend. He didn't want to say too much in front of you, because he realised that you were obviously more receptive to his ideas, but he was quite scathing about the whole thing, and there was no way he was going to ask for forgiveness for something that he didn't do. However, he did see the changes that happened with you, and as I held his hand in the quiet hospital ward that night, I could tell he was getting weaker. But then, for a brief moment, his eyes opened and he looked directly at me. It was like he was filled with some sort of energy force. He then spoke, softly and slowly, but quite clearly. He said he had finally asked for forgiveness and now did not have a fear of dying. He knew Christine and Julian were not far away and were waiting for him, and one day we would all be together again. And with that, he closed his eyes, and I knew he had gone."

Jenny's eyes filled with tears for a few moments. She tried to resist, but her very own words sent her into a period of grief-filled sobbing. Matt moved forward, holding and comforting his oldest friend. It was several minutes before she spoke again.

"Nancy, I am so sorry that it sounds like I'm excluding you from our group, but it's not the case at all. You are a dear friend whom I love and respect immensely."

"It's okay, Jenny. I didn't think that for one moment. Remember, I have parents who will be waiting for me, but then again, your biological parents might be waiting for you."

"And my daughter, along with two husbands. Now, that could be interesting, even potentially awkward."

Jenny was now gently laughing though her tears; it was a contagious chuckle that soon had Matt and Nancy joining in, as they thought of the potential humorous situation that it presented.

"Well, Jenny, I guess it all works out somehow, because numerous people have had multiple wives or husbands. But hopefully, we will all have a few more years on earth before we find out."

Nancy's honey-glazed chicken drumsticks and creamy vegetable casserole was a welcome sight for a hungry Jenny, whose day had started quite early. On returning to the sunroom and its panoramic view, it was quite noticeable how the crowds had swollen in the park below during their half hour in the dining room.

"Now I am going to hold back on the wine for a while, but before I have a break from the evil red stuff,

I would like to make a toast to John and Colin, the two men to whom we owe our freedom."

"To Colin and John."

The glasses clinked as the toast was made.

With her glass now firmly on the small table adjacent to her chair, Jenny continued the conversation. "I often wonder how things might have turned out if John was not to be trusted and had ended up double-crossing us."

"No, Jenny – don't even go down that path, as that never happened."

"Nancy, please. I know it didn't happen, but do hear me out."

It was obvious that Nancy didn't want to hear how events could have unfolded, but she courteously let Jenny have her say.

"I have been thinking – what if John had been collaborating with the bad guys, what would have happened? I can only guess that we would have been killed and both Matt and Adam would be locked away somewhere, never to see the light of day again."

"Yes, that probably would have happened."

"But worse still, have either of you ever considered what would have happened if John were collaborating with the people that Dr Hintermann was working for?"

"No, I haven't."

"I have, and it scares me a bit. We know what was left of that government department has been shut down, but what about the other lot? Are they still out there?

And if they are, then are they still trying to create superhumans, like the Nazis tried to create the perfect Aryan race?"

Nancy walked over to put her hand on Jenny's shoulder in an act of reassurance before speaking. "We have heard nothing from them since that night at the farm, so they are long gone out of our lives. John turned out to be a good man who was to be trusted and was able to expose all that had happened in the agency."

Jenny nodded in agreement. "Thank God for that. Now that you brought John up, there is something that I now find funny concerning him. It was when we arranged to meet him in that car park; however, it certainly wasn't funny at the time. I remember seeing his car pull up, with its tinted windows. My heart was thumping as I realised that if it were full of armed government agents, there was nothing that we could do because it would all be over. When John got out and walked towards us with his blank stare and lack of any emotion, I remember saying quietly to myself, 'Please, God, don't let it end like this.' Little did I know at the time that John was just as scared as we were, not knowing if he had been set up. I remember his look of relief when I answered his questions about Vern to the point that he realised I was telling the truth, and of course, our sense of relief when he said, 'It's okay; we'll get this sorted out.'"

"I know exactly what you mean, Jenny. My heart was beating so fast, I thought it was just about to burst out of my chest, but in all honesty, I was resigned to our fate, whatever it was. I knew that either way, good or bad, there would be no more running. So thank God it all turned out okay in the end, apart, of course, from–"

"It's okay, Nancy. We don't need to hide away from talking about Adam's death. Adam died protecting us. Because of him, we are free."

"I am sorry, Jenny. My sentence just didn't come out right."

There was a moment of awkward silence before Matt changed the subject.

"Jenny, you never got around to telling us the full story about your conversation with the staff at the old folks' home, when you went to contact Colin again."

"You're right! So much has happened since the funeral, and there hasn't really been the opportunity, but now is the perfect time. After John assured us that it really was all over, I realised there were things I needed to talk to someone about. There was so much Colin had talked of that I needed to find out more about. I needed to talk about Adam and where exactly he or his spirit was now.

"I rang and got put through to the head nurse, but when I asked to speak to Colin, there was silence. She eventually told me that Colin had passed away some time before. She asked who I was, and I told her I was a friend who had been to see him at the home, to which she replied, "Then you must be one of the group of four people who came to see him." Surprised by that, I asked her how she knew, and her answer surprised me even more. I remember Colin told us that he didn't get many visitors. Well, the nurse told me that in all the time that Colin was at the home, we were the only visitors he ever had. Evidently, Colin's four visitors were the talk of the whole home that week.

"We then talked for a while, and she told me that Colin was a changed man after we left that day. It was like he was totally at peace, as if his life had become complete and he had no reason to stay on earth. She also said his passing was very peaceful and it was only three days after our visit. When she told me, I suddenly realised what he'd meant when he said money was running out!

"Evidently, Colin's funeral was a very quiet event, with only a few of people from the home in attendance. They'd wanted to contact us but didn't have a clue as to who we were."

"That is really sad" Matt noted, "he must have had hundreds of people over the years in his congregation, so why did he not have any visitors? Or why did the home not have any contacts for him?"

"I wondered that very same thing, and the other thing that doesn't make any sense is why he was living at an old folk's home so far from where he came from? I even suspect he deliberately distanced himself from the people he knew, but all the time, he was waiting for us to call."

"Thank God we did. I know you said you had a lucky break, but you were able to find Colin! I am sure if someone else really wanted to find him, they could have. I know he had no family, but even so, you would have thought that someone would have wanted to see him. Remember what I said about that place when we were outside? I said it was like a place to leave people and forget about them."

The hands of the clock on the wall seemed to move quickly as the conversation flowed, there was so much catching up to do and so many memories to share. Nancy listened so intently to Matt and Jenny's descriptions of growing up in Mason that she could almost picture herself playing on the grounds of the orphanage. Jenny had always had an exceptionally good memory, and her prompts of names and events bought back many long-lost memories for Matt; some sad, a few unpleasant, but mostly happy. Matt and Jenny agreed that they might have been considered by some to have been disadvantaged by not having a real family, but in reality, they were one big family.

Nancy also shared a lot of her history and her exploits as a young girl. The flowing wine gave even the most mundane story a degree of humour. The subject of names also arose, with Matt now having four and Nancy three. Jenny noted that he might have had a fifth, as surely, his mother must have had a name for him, even if it was just 'baby boy'.

It was not till the final hour of the twentieth century that Jenny was ready to share her future plans.

"I think I have had enough wine to share with you what I am planning to do. Remember what you said about a new start? Well, I am going to have a new start now, too. I am going back to France."

"You're what. . ?"

"I thought you would be pleased for me."

"We are, but – well. . . that's unexpected. And we will miss you."

"And I will miss the both of you as well, but it is time to move on. I have been in contact with my friend Heidi. Jean Michel was a friend of her husband, Marc, and went to school with him. We all got on very well and spent quite a bit of time together. Well, Heidi and Marc were very supportive after the accident, but they divorced two years ago, and once all of their matrimonial affairs were sorted, Heidi ended up with their boutique hotel and café in a small village very close to the Swiss border. Now this is where it gets exciting. Her manager is retiring in early March, and she has asked me if I would like to take the position. I will work alongside the existing manager until she retires so I can get to know how everything works. I will have an income and somewhere to live and call home. In addition, the money I got from Adam's compensation will see me right for a while. Well then, what do you think? Are you excited for me?"

"Of course we are! That sounds like a great opportunity, and we're really pleased for you – but we will miss you."

"Thanks, but just think – you can come visit me and have somewhere to stay when you do. But wait, it gets even better. In late July, Heidi and I are going to have eight weeks driving around Europe in a camper van. The current manager has agreed to come back to cover for me. We are looking at starting in and going right through Scandinavia then working our way down to and finishing in Spain and Portugal. Can you imagine the fun we are going to have, two, single, middle-aged ladies in a campervan with lots of wine? Those Spanish men had better watch out!"

"It sounds like fun, but... I have to be honest. It doesn't sound like the Jenny that I know," Matt stated.

"Well, maybe not the old Jenny you knew. You two have each other, but I have no family left. We've both lost three good friends, but I have also lost a daughter and two husbands. I'm still healthy and young enough to create a new future for myself and maybe even have a bit of fun along the way, but I am nearly fifty-two, and I realise that I haven't got the seemingly endless years ahead that I had when I was younger.

"Both Heidi and I married young. I have no regrets for having the life that I did, and given the opportunity, I would do it all over again. I would give anything to have Jean Michel, Louise or Adam back, but they have all been taken from me, and my life can never be the same. So maybe it's time to do the things that I never did when I was younger and just let my hair down, and after what I have been through, what is the worst possible thing that can happen? I can just picture myself and Heidi driving around, both of us with dyed blonde hair, designer sunglass and flirting with all the young guys."

Jenny could not hide the smile that the thought provoked, but she eventually finished her thought. "Coming back to States, I was filled with so much anticipation. I didn't know who would turn up or what surprises the future would hold, and boy, what a time it has been. I now have that same feeling of anticipation about going back. What surprises will be waiting for me in Europe? Shortly, it will be not only a new year but also a new millennium, and if that is not the cue to do something totally different, then what is?"

"I can't argue with anything you've said, and I do wish you all the best. I know you will make a success of your venture and you will have a great time with your friend in the campervan."

"Thanks, Matt. I really appreciate what you said. Do you realise the irony of the situation that we're currently in? Thirty-four years ago, we were also drinking wine and waiting for the New Year's Eve fireworks display to commence, and I had just told you that I was going to France, like now – so who says that history never repeats? I know that there are still fifteen minutes to go, but happy New Year, happy new millennium and happy new lives."

Jenny raised her glass into the air.

"To our friends and family who can't be with us tonight."

Three glasses, now raised, clinked together simultaneously.